AESOP
LAKE

AESOP LAKE

A NOVEL

Sarah Ward

GREEN WRITERS PRESS *Brattleboro, Vermont*

Printed in the United States

10 9 8 7 6 5 4 3 2 1

Green Writers Press is a Vermont-based publisher whose mission is to
spread a message of hope and renewal through the words and images we
publish. Throughout we will adhere to our commitment to preserving and
protecting the natural resources of the earth. To that end, a percentage of our
proceeds will be donated to environmental activist groups. Green Writers
Press gratefully acknowledges support from individual donors, friends, and
readers to help support the environment and our publishing initiative.

Giving Voice to Writers & Artists Who Will Make the World a Better Place
Green Writers Press | Brattleboro, Vermont • www.greenwriterspress.com

ISBN: 978-0-9994995-2-8

PRINTED ON PAPER WITH PULP THAT COMES FROM FSC-CERTIFIED FORESTS, MANAGED FORESTS
THAT GUARANTEE RESPONSIBLE ENVIRONMENTAL, SOCIAL, AND ECONOMIC PRACTICES BY LIGHTNING
SOURCE ALL WOOD PRODUCT COMPONENTS USED IN BLACK & WHITE, STANDARD COLOR, OR SELECT
COLOR PAPERBACK BOOKS, UTILIZING EITHER CREAM OR WHITE BOOKBLOCK PAPER, THAT ARE
MANUFACTURED IN THE LA VERGNE, TENNESSEE PRODUCTION CENTER ARE
SUSTAINABLE FORESTRY INITIATIVE® (SFI®) CERTIFIED SOURCING.

Dedicated to
Lindsay
for giving voice to the lambs,
warming the world with your rays,
and standing in unity with others.

CONTENTS

✦

PART THREE: UNITY

Part One

THE BULLY

✦

THE
HUNGRY WOLF
AND
THE LAMB

A STRAY LAMB stood on the bank of a stream lapping up water, unaware of a gray wolf standing upstream.

"Perfect," said the wolf. "There is my meal, foolishly wandering off by itself."

"Hey there, little lamb. What do you mean by muddying up my drinking water?" he growled.

"I'm sorry," said the lamb, "but I'm not muddying up the water! I'm using only the tip of my tongue, and besides, I'm downstream from you."

"Don't argue with me," the wolf snarled. "I know all about you. You've been going around telling everyone that I'm no good. You are the problem, and I should take care of you right now."

"That can't be," the small lamb protested.

"Well," snapped the wolf, "if it wasn't you, it was your father, and that is just as bad."

And before the lamb could say another word, the wolf sprang on the poor creature and ate him up.

A bad excuse is good enough for a bully.

1

✦

Leda Keogh

THE WOLF

AVID AND I rip down the gravel road toward
the town reservoir in a black pickup truck. The
windows are down, and the air blows in hot
as if it were a steamy summer evening instead of May.
My short brown hair is becoming a tangled mess, but
I don't care. The air smells yellow like summer though
the forsythias have bloomed and faded. The ferns grow
thick on the forest floor and David reeks of motor oil
and sweat. I turn my head towards him, following his
scent with animal instinct. His tousled black hair and
chiseled chin bring out the Italian on his mother's side,
while his stocky, short frame is all Portuguese, according
to his mother.

We fit perfectly together, though David's shoulders, broad from lifting weights for baseball, can lift my
skinny ass up over his head like a bale of hay. I tip my
nose toward my armpit and notice that my deodorant

has stopped working. The water will help us wash clean. I want to be with David tonight, to make up with him after our fight. I want him to know I'm not mad at him. It was stupid, really. He was just being a guy, cruising around the school like a rutting moose. He didn't really hurt anyone, just made stupid jokes. Misplaced jealousy, that's all it was.

I had smiled and giggled and waved goodbye to Ricky as I left chemistry lab, forgetting David was going to walk me to art class. Forgetting he sees green when I even talk to another guy. It doesn't matter if that guy is dating someone else, or in this case, is gay. David saw it happen and pulled me to the side as I left the classroom—then waited for Ricky to exit. He looped his arm with mine and stepped us into the wave of students, walking directly behind Ricky, taunting him under his breath, calling Ricky a fairy. He was mad all afternoon.

"Do you think the water will be cold?" I ask.

"Should be cold enough." He reaches over and pinches my left nipple. My cheeks burn, but I don't move away, just hold my arms in tighter to my sides as he starts laughing. I push the uncomfortable feeling away and let his smile make me feel better.

The gravel under the tires crackles as we pull into the parking lot of the reservoir. Voices are coming from the dark water, and the occasional splash echoes through the trees. Someone is probably jumping off the dam into the thirty-foot black water. I wonder again how cold it is. Probably better to just jump and get it over with, otherwise I might chicken out. The thought of being naked in the icy water makes me blush again, and then I see the other car. Damn.

"Come on, David. Let's get out of here," I urge. "I don't want to take my clothes off in front of people and I didn't bring a suit."

"Let's just see who it is," he insists, parking the 4x4. David doesn't acknowledge the silver Beetle parked under the trees, but I know it's Ricky and Jonathan. I don't really care that they're gay, and for the most part it doesn't really affect me. Ricky and I do labs together. He's smart, pretty funny, gentle, and very, very gay. When a beautiful, doe-eyed boy looks dreamily at his best friend, you can tell they're not just friends.

"I don't want to skinny dip with other people around, David, and I don't have a suit. Let's just go." I'm begging now, but he is already out the door, closing it quietly. I climb out and sidle up, grabbing his hand, which he squeezes.

The moonlight strikes the water, lighting up the silhouette of two boys with their arms wrapped tightly around each other. They're making out near one of the big boulders lining the shore. Ricky's smaller physique against Jonathan's makes him look almost feminine, but the squareness of their shoulders, the flat chests and narrow waists, gives them away.

"Let's go, David," I whisper. I can see his chest heaving. His anger is a python, squeezing the warmth from the air.

"What the fuck!" he snaps, shifting back and forth on his feet. "Those fucking faggots are messing up our spot! What the fuck are they doing?"

I pull David by the arm back towards the pickup.

"Come on, David, let's go. I don't really care if we can't swim tonight. We can come back another time."

He lets me drag him away, back down the path and to the truck. I'm relieved. Then he reaches into his pocket and pulls out his phone. Before I know what's happening, I hear him talking to MJ.

"You gotta get over to the dam, dude. We got ourselves a couple of pansies doing the nasty. . . . Yeah, no shit. Are you coming or what?"

I raise my hand to cover my shocked mouth.

He looks up at me. "What?"

"Why are you doing this?" An urge to scream out to Ricky and Jonathan rises. I know MJ only lives a mile and a half down the road. He'll be here any minute.

"Why am I doing what? Is one of them your gay BFF?" He raises his voice high and flicks out a pinky.

I stare at David for a long moment, and he stares back, daring me to challenge him. My heart pounds in my chest, and I drop my gaze. David steps closer and places his large hand on the back of my thigh, pulling me close.

"This," he says, pulling my body up against him, "this is what is meant to happen between a man and a woman." He leans in, pressing me between his hips and the cold metal of his truck. I don't move or breathe. I can't.

I hear tires on gravel, and MJ pulls up in his mother's Suburban. He jumps out. David turns away from me as if nothing is happening. I take a step away from the truck bed, trying to act as if everything is fine. My stomach does a flip as I see what MJ is holding.

"What are you doing?" I ask. MJ looks down at his shotgun.

"This? It's just for show." And David starts snickering, his dark hair cutting across his beautiful eyes. David catches my expression, and suddenly he knows exactly what I'm going to do. He grabs me by the arm and digs in his fingers.

"Don't spoil all our fun," he whispers. "We aren't going to hurt them, Leda. No one is going to get hurt. I promise. Get in the truck and wait for us," he commands. "Can I trust you?" he asks. "Because if I can't, I'm sure the cops would love to hear about your mom."

My gut tightens into my chest. I nod, exhaling. He slowly relaxes his grip.

"Just stay here. We won't take long, just a little scare." His voice is steady. He and MJ move down to the water.

I back away towards the door of the truck and feel for the cool, worn handle. I clamber up to the passenger's seat and squint into the darkness.

A shot rings out and someone's scream breaks through the dense air of the cab. There is splashing, shouting. Then another shot and more screams. My heart is pounding. I pull my phone from my jeans. Tears slide out of the corners of my eyes. I wipe them quickly away and slide to the floor of the truck.

2

✦

Jonathan Tanner-Eales
THE LAMB

THE GRASSY BEACH that meets the water is empty of families. They've gone home, I suppose, to heat up leftovers and watch their favorite Thursday-night sitcom. I stare at Ricky for a long moment and then gulp the air and dive below the surface, challenging him to hold his breath. I resurface and fill my lungs, aching to reach out towards him.

"Ricky, you suck at holding your breath. You need to work out more, build your endurance," I tease.

"Oh yeah?" he says. "Then come over here and show me how it's done." Ricky's blond hair is plastered to his head. His skin stays a copper tan all year long, as if he surfed the ocean blue. He dives beneath the dark water and disappears. I wait for him to resurface, recalling the reasons I love him.

He's so brainy, especially with science. He's taken every AP science class Mount Lincoln offers, and he tutors freshmen, a gig he keeps to himself. In our hick town, it's not cool to like musicals, or be too smart. We both want out.

Darkness cloaks the woods that encircle the reservoir. The trees are now black sentries in formation, and for a moment I think I hear the sound of a door slam in the distance. Then I feel the movement of the water and Ricky's hand reaching toward me. My pulse quickens, every muscle on edge and ready for his touch.

When I met Ricky, I was staying under wraps, blending in—well except for my blue hair and pierced lip—but I kept to myself, and then pow, the air was sucked out of the room. Angels sang and a gentle wind blew through the auditorium doors, carrying a small-framed boy with blond curls and mocha eyes. It wasn't just a sexual thing—though that was there, electric, a force that pulled me to touch him. I felt an instant connection, a comforting one, like I was meant to know him. It would have been so easy to just reach out and place my hand on the back of this boy's collar, and I knew we would melt together. When Ricky turned his face toward me, our eyes met and his face lit up, happiness and wariness all twisted together.

Our friendship developed quickly and we hung out after play rehearsal, studied together on the weekends, and met up in the cafeteria for lunch. With Ricky, I could express my fascination with films, the choreography, the cinematography, everything. He knows I want to be a great director. I want to bring musicals back to film. He knows I used to take private dance lessons, and that I memorized the lines and songs of every musical written by Rodgers and Hammerstein. My escape, when my parents gave each other the silent treatment, was to plug in the headphones and learn a new musical score. Ricky listens and encourages my dreams, and I encourage his.

It wasn't long before we noticed the smirks and laughter as we walked through the hallway together. It should have been okay. After all, the school has a Pride Club. But that didn't stop David and his jock buddies, with their macho-righteous attitudes. They would block our passage into, or worse, out of the bathroom. When you're trapped and scared and expect a quick knee to the groin, and then everyone goes their own way, you know who owns the school. No teacher saying, "Watch it, boys." Just the guys having fun.

It's so rare that Ricky and I find time to be alone. Mom is always home, writing in her office, and Ricky's family, though they know he is gay, is not so accepting that he is also a sexual being. Ricky and I were told that under no circumstances were we to hang out in his bedroom. No such rules for Ricky's older sister, Anita. Apparently being gay means being celibate. But his mom never said we couldn't go swimming together.

When Ricky emerges, I wrap my arms around his waist and place my lips on his, tasting the water. Finally touching. I want him to feel the heat running through my blood. He stands in front of a boulder at the edge of the shoreline and I ease him back against it, kissing his neck. Ricky lets out a sigh of relief and exhilaration.

I hear a blast and something ricochets off the rock next to Ricky's back. I'm so confused. I hear hollering in the distance, and then screaming in my ear. I look down. It's coming from Ricky. Someone is yelling, something about queers, but I can't understand it. I can't make out any faces, just the shape of two people.

I grab Ricky's hand and pull him out into the water, his legs moving like the tin man.

"Are you okay?" I ask. Ricky's face is terror-stricken. His eyes are bulging and he stares straight ahead.

"Come on. We have to swim away, *now*." I try to pull Ricky into the deeper water. His arms and legs will not move. The white witch has turned him to stone. He just stands there, knee deep.

"I'm going to teach two queens a lesson," a voice declares, moving closer.

"Jesus, Ricky, we have to get out of here. Someone is coming. We have to swim away," I plead, but nothing snaps Ricky out of it. Hot tears run down my cheeks. Desperation clutches my heart. I have seen enough movies to know this is not going to end well.

"Leave us alone!" I shout toward the voices. I reach out and slap Ricky across the face. Maybe it will shake him into action. Another shot, and I feel sharp pain in my thigh and butt, like bee stings. My hands instinctively move over my crotch. My thigh is numb. Ricky begins to shake uncontrollably. He is the lamb waiting for the wolf. Someone stands at the edge of the reservoir and I can see the barrel of a gun pointed in our direction. Another guy moves quickly into the water towards us and reaches out. He grabs Ricky's arm from his statue of a body.

"No!" I yell, and grab at any part of Ricky I can, trying to keep him away and safe. But I can't hang on to his wet body, and I can't let myself be pulled up the embankment with him. He's being pulled out of my reach. My empty hands swipe the air where Ricky's body should be.

I turn towards the water, gulp air, and dive deep and far. My mind is racing for an idea of what to do. I can't fight them. Ricky isn't here. He has disappeared. I push myself through the water as far from the shore as I can until my lungs feel as if they will explode. My head breaks the surface, and I gasp for air.

"So, you're a faggot and a pussy," the voice hollers. Another round of pellets sprays the water to my left.

Ricky's pale body levitates out of the water and lands on the edge of the bank like a mannequin. The shadows move closer. They kick him. He hardly reacts. It looks like they're pulverizing a log. He doesn't cry out, or twist away. Their boots thump against him and they laugh.

"Come on out and help your boyfriend, faggot!" a voice yells. "We already fucked him up, there's not much left for you." They break into laughter. I keep my legs moving, try to slow my breathing, and swallow the sobs. A light comes on in the distance and I wonder if someone has reported a disturbance.

"Come on, let's go," I hear one of them suggest. "If he doesn't get the message, we'll find him alone."

"Yeah, okay." The other is bent over and grabs something off the shoreline. Then his arm flings back and I hear a splash to my left. God, I hope that's not my phone.

"Did you hear that, fucker? We'll get you next time!" the first voice yells.

I stay in the water, feeling the milfoil against my legs. Doors slam. There's more yelling, and then the rip of tires against the gravel. I move through the cold water to the edge of the bank. My body is covered in goose-bumps and my legs ache. My mind feels numb, but all my anger is hot in my gut. I know I need to get out of the water, so I find my footing and heave my body onto the grassy slope.

Ricky looks like clay, muted and misshapen. I can't see any movement, and for a split second I believe the worst. Tears sting my eyes and snot drips from my nose. I reach out to touch his skin. I can feel his chest moving. "Thank god," I whisper.

"Hey, Ricky. It's me, Jonathan. Can you hear me? They're gone." I want to reassure him. My voice breaks and tears stream down my face. I'm afraid to touch him. I want him to know it's going to be okay, so I wrap my arms around his shoulders and lean my head against his chest.

"I'm right here. I'm not going anywhere." My head lifts and drops in time to Ricky's breathing. He needed me and I didn't help. I should have tried. I should have forced him into the water with me. Maybe I could have knocked that guy off balance. I feel like I'm going to retch.

3

✦

Leda Keogh

UPSTREAM

GET OUT. That is the answer. Get out of the truck and leave. Don't be a part of this. Then I can call the police, or someone. Leave an anonymous tip. I slip from the floor of the truck to the ground and quietly close the door. I can still hear splashing, and screaming, more shouting. MJ fires his shotgun and laughs. My mother's watery blue eyes reflect back to me in the side-view mirror. If I call the police, David will tell them about my mom. It could be enough to get her locked away. I picture my mother wearing a gray prison uniform, thin and wasting away in a cell.

And then I start running as fast and as far as I can. I take the south road, not the direction the boys will take when they leave. They will drive the north road back to MJ's house. My gut spews lava into my throat, making it ache. I want someone to help, to keep me safe. Maybe I'd be braver if I had someone with me. I slow and look at my phone: 11:32 P.M. It's a solid hour hike back to my house from here. What if I have Keegan come get me? Would he tell Mom? The phone rings twice.

"Keegan?"

"Hey, what's up little sister?" His voice is groggy; he must have fallen asleep early tonight. My voice cracks open, and I want to tell him everything. My chest aches, I'm breathing hard, and I know I have to keep walking fast. I keep looking back over my shoulder.

"Can you come get me?" I huff.

"Are you okay?" His voice echoes my distress. I don't usually call from a date looking for a ride home.

"Uh, well," I manage. "I need a ride."

"Where are you?"

I look around to assess my surroundings. "I'm at the bottom of South Street, just about a half mile from the dam. I don't want to wait on the side of the road. I'll meet you by the Hansen's garage, okay?"

"Leda, what the hell? I thought you were with David? Did he hurt you?"

"No, it's okay. I'll explain when you get here, just . . . Keegan?"

"What?"

"Don't tell Mom, okay?"

"Are you nuts? She's not even here. God knows when she'll be back."

It's darker here at the edge of the woods and I think I see shadows move in the thick of the trees. I can't hear the chaos at the water anymore. Maybe it's over. Then I think about the screams and the gunshots. I think about Ricky. He's beautiful. If he weren't gay, he'd have some zillion girls chasing after him. Some of the freshmen still do, until he walks by them, his hand tethered to Jonathan's elbow. It's odd, Ricky was never really out until Jonathan moved from Boston last year. I don't really know Jonathan. He's definitely a city boy: different clothes, blue hair, a pierced lip. He made an impression his first day in skin-tight jeans and T-shirt.

I see the Hansen's house up ahead. It will stand empty until June, when they return for the summer from Florida. If they knew how warm this May is, they'd probably be back sooner. I'm grateful the house is empty. Thick shrubs snake around the garage and I tuck myself into them.

Lights flash down the road from the direction of the reservoir. My heart sinks. I push myself farther into the shrubs, inhaling their pungent odor, and watch as a white car zooms past.

When I was little, our family went camping in the Green Mountains. That was when my dad was alive. He took Keegan, Mom, and me up to the mountains to teach us to survive in the woods. Dad knew everything about surviving in the wilderness. He wanted us to know how to find food from the forest and how to tell direction by looking on which side of the tree the moss grows. He read from survival manuals and tested us on the names of poisonous plants, how to build a bridge, and the best place to raise a tent and keep out the cold. I loved these expeditions, and my mother hated them. She left the quests up to my brother and me, disappearing into our tent to study for her nursing degree, which she never completed.

When I was seven and Keegan was twelve, I answered the door to a man in a uniform. He wore black shoes that looked just like my dad's. The officer asked for my mother. I remember staring out at the blue flashing lights and hearing my mother crying. I heard the mumbled words, something about black ice and car pileups. Dad's car was destroyed by an eighteen-wheeler coming back from a trip to Pittsburgh.

I kept thinking he would let us ride in his police car on the way to the hospital. I could see my father, and then I would tell him about our ride with the lights flashing and a siren. The police officer just put his hands on my shoulders and moved me aside so he could leave the house. When I turned around, my mother was staring at a business card. Apparently, it was the address where we could collect my father's remains.

My knees begin to ache as I stand pressed into the scratchy shrubs. My black tank top and jean shorts are doing little to protect against the mosquitoes. When Keegan's car finally arrives, I feel light-headed with relief. I climb into the front seat, tasting blood from biting my lip.

"You look like shit." He gives me a challenging look, as if to say, *Don't try to lie to me.*

"Thanks, nice to see you too," I say, looking at his straight brown hair poking up in all directions. He reaches a finger up to his green eyes to dislodge a sleepy seed, and for just a moment we are seven and twelve again, and I don't want to tell him what went down. But then he readjusts, filling the driver's seat, and turns to me.

"What happened?" he asks, crossing his long arms as if he is not going to drive me anywhere until I tell him exactly what happened. He looks just like Dad when he does this, and my heart aches just a little bit.

"It's kind of a long story. Can you just get us out of here first?" I plead, trying to see past his shoulder in the direction of the reservoir.

"Leda, what happened? What are you looking at?" He looks out the window as if he could conjure the scene inside my head.

"I really just need you to take me home. Now!" I yell, louder than I intend, and he looks surprised and worried, but pulls the car around.

I keep hearing the screams and wonder what actually happened to Ricky and Jonathan.

"Hey, what's up? Why are you so upset?" There is genuine concern in Keegan's voice now. Not the normal tolerance of my "girlyness," as he likes to refer to anything emotional. He pulls the car over and looks at me.

"I was with David; we went to the reservoir to hang out."

"Did he try to hurt you? Did he make you do something you didn't want to do?" Keegan flares and he's instantly ready to bust some skulls.

"No, it's nothing like that, it's just . . . well, when we got there, to the reservoir, another couple was there, and David, he kind of lost it."

"Because you didn't have the water to yourself? It's a public place, isn't it?"

"Not because of that." I hesitate. "He freaked out because the other couple was Ricky and Jonathan."

Keegan looks at me as if I had just said there were Martians at the reservoir.

"What were they doing?" he asks, and I raise my eyebrows knowingly.

"And David was a little disturbed?"

"No, David was a lot disturbed. He completely freaked out. He called MJ, who's just a complete thug."

"To do what?" Keegan asks.

"They decided to scare the boys. MJ showed up with a shotgun. It all got out of hand."

"So, what did they do?" Keegan asks, and I can see by the look in his eyes he's already guessed. He knows why I'm here and not there.

"I don't know, exactly. I started freaking out and David made me get back into the truck, but then I heard screaming and splashing and decided to run away. I got down the road and that's when I called you."

"Do you want to go back to the reservoir?" Keegan asks. "To check on Ricky and Jonathan?"

"I don't know. I guess so. Will they wonder what I'm doing there?" I should want to go find them. I didn't hurt them.

Keegan slowly turns the car around and drives towards the reservoir, mumbling to himself something about assholes.

"Oh shit," he says quietly, and pulls the car off to the edge of the road, looking into his rearview mirror.

"What?" I twist my head around and look behind us as an ambulance and a police cruiser race by. The lava reignites, bubbling in my gut. Keegan begins to move back onto the road.

"No, stop!" I shout.

He turns towards me. "Maybe I should just take you home?"

I nod, and fold myself into a ball on the front seat to cry.

4

✦

Jonathan Tanner-Eales

DOWNSTREAM

RICKY'S CHEST moves up and down, but sometimes his breath is uneven. His skin is cold and clammy. I need to tell someone where we are, to get help. What if Ricky stops breathing? My shaking hands search the ground around us, and I find a towel, stepped on but still somewhat dry. I wipe myself off and feel my thigh. I can't tell the difference between water and blood. What blood is still in my body is pounding in my ear. I need some clothes. I'm shivering and exposed as I reach between the shrubs for the clothes we removed earlier in the evening. It's a relief they didn't get taken. I pull on boxers and shorts, not sure whose are whose.

I've got to warm Ricky up somehow. I'm afraid to move him much, so I tilt his head a bit to ensure he is getting air and prop it in place with a sneaker. I lay the damp towel and put a shirt over Ricky. Will that be enough? Panic surges through me, but I push it away. I need to stay in control right now. Ricky is depending on me to get us out of this. I feel around the moist grass until my fingers touch the cold surface of my phone. I should call 911, but all I want is my mom.

"Hi, honey," she answers.

"Mom?" My voice cracks.

"Honey, what's wrong?"

"Mom, Ricky and I . . . we were attacked." And then I'm sobbing, as if saying it out loud makes it even more real.

"Attacked? What do you mean, honey? Tell me what happened. Where are you?" I can hear the panic in her voice.

"We're at the reservoir, by the dam. We were swimming, but some guys came along . . . Mom, they beat the shit out of Ricky. He's really hurt." I take a deep breath to try to gain some composure. I feel like a ten-year-old, not a senior in high school ready to head off to college.

"How bad is he, Jonathan? Do you need an ambulance? Jonathan, are you hurt?"

"I'm not sure. I'm mostly shook up, and my leg hurts. I think I was hit by a pellet."

"A shotgun? They were shooting at you with a shotgun? Oh my god." She sucks in her breath.

"Mom, can you come?" I beg.

"What? Of course. Oh, sweetie, of course. I'm on my way. I'm going to call 911 first and get some help, but I'm on my way. What about Ricky's parents?"

"No, I haven't called them yet," I confess, and feel a pang of guilt.

"Okay, listen, I'm going to call them on my way to the reservoir. I'll be there soon," she confirms, and then disconnects.

The moon has risen to its peak. Time stretches like the fog in the dark, and I feel betrayed by shadows. Every twig snap and surge of water onto the banks of the reservoir fills me with fear. My heart pummels my ears, and I inch closer to Ricky.

"Ricky, wake up and talk to me," I demand. I lie next to his bruised body, placing an arm carefully across his chest, breathing in sync with him, afraid to let go.

Bright red and blue emergency lights make the parking lot above us glow. Flashlights scan across the path above us and down towards the water. I reach up my hand to block my eyes. I've been trying to keep Ricky warm, pressed up against him, trying to keep myself warm too. Will they know what I'm doing? An urge to move away from Ricky's naked body overwhelms me, but I ignore it.

People in uniforms circle around us, telling me to "let go" and to "let us help," and I try to make sense of it all. I feel a tug under my arms as a man tries to pull the towel off from Ricky.

"He's been hurt," I tell them.

"We know, son, we're here to help," explains a soft voice. "But we have to take a look at him before we move him to this gurney. Do you understand?" It's a woman, but not my mom. Where is my mom? She said she would come right away.

"Are you injured?" she asks as her hands and someone else, a man I think, gently lift me up onto my feet. "Can you walk?" I nod, but then realize it's too dark for her to see. A heated blanket enfolds me, and flares illuminate the path to the top of the hill where the ambulance is parked. Blinking red and white lights guide the way. I hear lots of commotion behind us, but this woman with dark, curly hair escorts me away from the noise, away from Ricky.

"Wait, I need to stay with him," I say, panic rising again.

"The crew is taking care of him. It's okay. What's your name?"

"Jonathan."

"And your last name?"

"Tanner-Eales."

"Are you a senior at Mount Lincoln High? I think my daughter goes to school with you."

"Yeah."

"You were in the spring musical this year, right? The *Music Man*? Emma was on stage crew. You were really good." Her compliment sounds sincere, and some of my worry eases. This nice person won't let Ricky die.

"Thanks," I say.

Before I know what's happening, I'm sitting on a metal stool outside an ambulance. Emma's mother applies a swab, some salve, and gauze to my throbbing thigh. I watch her steady hands, and she goes on and on about the play, as if we were sitting in the cafeteria discussing my drama credits. Her voice is calming as she wraps a blood pressure gauge around my arm and pumps it tight. She releases the air in small bursts before letting all of the air loose and jotting numbers on a clipboard.

"That's a nice tattoo," she says, pointing to my right shoulder where two colorful drama masks have been layered into my skin. A pang of guilt floods me. I remember my mother's first view of them upon my return from spring break in Boston with my father. Since moving away, it had been easy to get my dad to agree to anything I wanted, even paying for me to consecrate my love for theatre. Mom was pissed and she used the opportunity to unleash a tirade on Dad filled with meaningless threats involving court orders and custody visits.

"Thanks," I say again, and pull the blanket back over my shoulders. What could be holding up my mom? She moves on to my pulse and my temperature, all the while asking about classes and teachers. Part of me wants to scream at her to cut it out, but it feels good not to think about what happened. For just a moment I can rest. My brain aches; my body aches.

"They'll check you over more at the hospital, but that should do it for now." Emma's mom raises her eyes to me. "I think Officer Templeton needs to speak with you over there by the boulders."

I follow her gaze to an officer in uniform taking pictures with a phone and jotting notes down on a pad of paper. She has straight black hair pulled back into a braid under her cap. Her name tag reflects in the flashing of the ambulance lights. The officer circles closer to the ambulance and looks up at us, anticipating an opportunity to begin her formal introduction.

"Jonathan Tanner-Eales?" She extends her hand to me. I respond with the expected handshake.

"Yes," I confirm, not sure how she knows my name.

"This is your car?" she says, pointing to my silver Beetle, "J-TAN" on the Mass plate.

"Yes," I confirm again.

"Can you tell me what happened here tonight?" Her voice is steady, but it puts me on notice. I'm suddenly aware that I'm making a police report, that my words could be used in a court of law. I don't want to think about it. I just want my mom. I begin to relay the story, describing the limited details that I have to offer from the darkness.

"Do you have any idea who they were?" she asks. I hesitate, knowing that I might be putting myself and Ricky in more danger.

"Even a guess?" the officer encourages me.

"Maybe David Slayton and his friend MJ." Then I see our Corolla pull into the parking lot, followed immediately by Ricky's parents' car.

"Mom!" I yell, and try to stand, but the officer gently pushes me back onto the rock.

"I think you should stay seated, Jonathan. Your mother will come and find you." But I'm too distracted to keep talking to this cop.

"Please," I beg, "I really need her." It comes out awkwardly, but I don't care. The officer gives me a concerned look and nods. I stand quickly, not waiting for her to change her mind.

"Jonathan? Are you okay?" I hear my mom's voice and see her arms outstretched and then I'm wrapping myself tightly around her, like the time I was seven and lost my way in the mall and was so relieved to find her. She holds tight. My face is buried in her auburn hair that's been pulled back into ponytail. Her head barely reaches my chin, but her embrace helps me to feel safe. When I let go, the officer steps forward and extends a hand.

"Hi, Ms. Tanner. My name is Officer Templeton. I've just been talking with your son here. I'd like to continue asking him some more questions at the hospital."

"He needs to go to the hospital?"

"Yes, to clean out his wounds, and we'll need to have him examined as a part of the investigation." The word investigation lingers in the air between all of us. Of course this is a criminal case. Officer Templeton is rambling on about evidence and corroboration of the stories with the evidence.

"Can I drive him to the hospital?" Mom asks.

"Actually, I'll be driving Jonathan," Officer Templeton explains. "I'll need to keep him with me until we're able to corroborate his story with the doctors. It's safer for him. Do you understand?"

Mom nods, but the lines in her forehead multiply. "Are you trying to insinuate that my son did this to his boyfriend?"

I turn to look at Officer Templeton. Why would they think that?

She turns towards my mother and lowers her voice.

"No, ma'am, but I need to follow protocol. Your son and I have talked about suspects, but the strongest case I can build against them will include clearing Jonathan of all possible suspicion, and we need a medical exam to do that." Her logic makes sense, and I relax a little. "I'll give you a few minutes together. But we should head to the hospital soon."

Ricky is already in the rescue wagon, and his mom

Rita is climbing aboard with him. Alan, his father, is getting into their car to follow.

My mother turns to me. "Honey, I know this has been a nightmare for you. I want to help and I think Officer Templeton is right. You need to stay with her until we get you to the hospital. I'll drive right behind and meet you at the door of the ER, okay?"

"Mom?" My eyes brim with fresh tears. "Mom, I couldn't protect him. I tried to get Ricky to swim away with me, but I couldn't. He just froze up."

"Oh, honey. It's not your fault. I'm sure you did what you could."

"But what if he's not okay? What if he . . ." The words won't leave my mouth.

"Sweetie, we just have to wait and see. Let's go to the ER to get you looked at, and then we can ask about Ricky, okay?" She steers me towards Officer Templeton, who is holding the door open to her cruiser. I climb into the hard, black plastic seat. There's wire mesh between me and the front seat. My mother tugs at the corners of the blanket to pull it more tightly around my shoulders and kisses my cheek. Her green eyes stare into mine for a long moment. When she closes the door, I am alone.

Officer Templeton climbs into the driver's seat and another officer who I don't know shifts into the passenger seat directly in front of me. He turns around to look at me.

"You okay back there?" he asks.

I shrug. "I guess," I whisper.

"Bet you wished you and your friend stayed home, huh?" the officer asks.

"Leave him alone, Jeff."

"I'm just saying. It's a public place, that's all."

I don't respond, just feel a familiar silence heating up the cruiser.

My mom meets me near the door to Urgent Care. The antiseptic atmosphere of the Vermont Medical Center is overwhelming. Perky lights do their best to send a cheerful welcome to the hurt and injured. My injuries don't meet the criteria for emergency, so instead we are shuffled over to the urgent care waiting room. Ricky was probably rushed into the ER through the back corridor. I know he is being assessed somewhere. I need to know what's going on and if he's responding.

On one side of the room, families wait with their crying children. Puzzles and games are stacked in the corner and a television tuned to PBS shows *The Cat in the Hat*. On the other side, empty chairs line the wall, magazines sit stiffly on a coffee table, and a TV blasts CNN—because of course sick and injured people need to know there are more sick and injured people in the world. It's a hopelessly ugly space. If I were to design an emergency room waiting area, it would be set up like a spa: soft lights, waves crashing, birds gathering, that kind of thing. Maybe a few massage chairs for people waiting on news.

I look around the room. A man in his mid-twenties sits across from us with an ice pack on his head and cuts on his cheek and hands. Maybe a minor farming accident—he looks like he works outside. A gray-haired woman is reading a magazine. She doesn't seem to have anything wrong with her, but she keeps looking up every time someone moves at the reception desk or opens a door. She's probably waiting for someone.

At the reservoir, Rita never once looked at me. It was like she didn't want to acknowledge I was with her son. Maybe because Ricky was only covered in blankets, no clothes. It's one thing to have a gay son, but now they have a gay son, probably outed in the papers and on the news, making the headlines because he was beaten up.

"I want to go in and see Ricky." My mother nods and gets up to speak to the receptionist.

"Can you tell me the status of Ricky Norton?" she asks. I watch the balding man behind the desk search a computer screen for the right name.

"He's still being assessed, ma'am. Are you friend or family?"

"Friends," she replies.

"They're only letting family in to see him at this point. That will probably change once he's admitted and they have a room for him to receive visitors."

By the time I'm brought into my own exam room and the nurse has taken my vitals, I feel like I'm in a downward spiral. I'm so tired. I lie on the gurney and the fluorescent lights radiate off me. The television screen flickers with reruns of *How I Met Your Mother*. The characters move in and out of spaces, bar scenes, a living room.

It's two in the morning. I ask anyone who walks into my room how Ricky is and learn nothing. Instead they ask me questions about my wounds and apply antiseptics and gauze, telling me how lucky I am. I turn my face away. Finally, Ricky's father appears at the door. He is a tall, thin, balding man with Ricky's eternal tan and brown eyes. I bolt upward and pain shoots down my leg.

"Jonathan? Can I come in?" He has dark circles under his eyes and worry lines in his forehead that look as though they have been permanently etched into his face. Mom rises and offers Mr. Norton her chair next to the gurney, but he declines with a shake of his head. He enters the room, but just barely.

"I wondered if you could tell me what happened tonight? I mean, I know you've talked to the police, and the doctors, and have given them all the details you can. But I need to hear them for myself," Mr. Norton says.

So, for the third time in two hours, I recount the evening's events, leaving out some of the more intimate details for Mr. Norton's benefit, because really, what parent wants to hear the details of their child's intimate activities? Mr. Norton isn't comfortable even when Ricky and I just hang out together. He disappears into his workshop, where he makes wooden picnic tables, benches, and toys to sell. It seems to me he spends more time with his tools than with Ricky. We haven't shared many conversations for that reason, and I feel awkward talking about my date with his son, but his face is pleading, so I inhale and begin.

For some reason it feels different to tell the story to Mr. Norton. I'm cold again and feel myself shaking. "I couldn't help him, Mr. Norton," I say, pleading with him to understand. "I tried to get him to swim away with me. I thought if we could swim across the reservoir to the other side then we would be safe, that we could run through the woods and escape. But Ricky just froze, his whole body went stiff, and he screamed when the first shot hit the rocks, but after that he didn't say anything."

Mr. Norton blinks and tears slide down his cheek. He reaches a hand up to wipe them away. I keep explaining because I can't think of anything else to do. When I finish, there is silence and I wonder if Mr. Norton is ever going to speak.

"I suppose you know I've never been fond of Ricky's . . . ah, preference," Mr. Norton says. "Not that I don't like you, Jonathan, but it's been hard, and I've struggled with how to be a father to a boy like Ricky." He pauses and looks around at the room, the figures on the TV screen, and then down at his hands. "I thought the world had changed, and I've tried to change. And now . . ." he chokes up and swallows, "now Ricky's face, and . . . I hate myself for not letting him know he's important to me. That it doesn't matter." He goes silent, eyes leaking. Mom steps forward and puts her hand on Mr. Norton's arm.

"You'll be able to tell him, Alan. He just needs time to recover."

Mr. Norton nods at her and then looks to me.

"Thank you for not abandoning him. I'm grateful to you." With that, he steps into the hallway and I sit in the wake of his grief, wondering what to do next.

5

✦

Leda Keogh

PACK ANIMALS

When I wake the next morning everything looks normal. The same beige curtains block out the strongest rays of the sun. My easel stands in the corner with this week's painting, a still life of fruit in a bowl. Paintbrushes and oil paints are spread all over my desk. My windowpane, which has a small crack that needs repair, allows cool air to waft around me, and I snuggle deeper. Everything feels safe here, except for the fact that I can still hear screams echoing off water.

Keegan and I arrived last night to an empty house. Keegan said it would be better to just go home and not get involved. Ricky and Jonathan wouldn't know I was there, only David and MJ would, and why would they want an eyewitness? Mom came home shortly after I turned my light out. I heard her open my door and look in on me, checking to see if I was in bed. She always wants to seem like more of a mother than she is.

I wonder if Jonathan and Ricky will be at school today. If they know who it was, they will tell someone. The memory of the ambulance passing us causes my stomach to lurch. Oh god, what if they were seriously injured? My feet are weights as I move into the bathroom and turn the shower knob. Could I have stopped it? Why didn't I call the police? I think back to the month before, when our home was broken into. We were coming home after eating dinner at the café. The door was ajar, and the contents of our living room were strewn everywhere. Keegan dashed into the house and turned lights on, as if this would alert the intruder to our presence, but I shrunk back and waited for Mom and Keegan to tell me what to do. Slowly, Mom and I made our way through the house. The only rooms touched were the living room, my mother's bedroom, and her bathroom. Bureau drawers in her room were emptied and the contents of her medicine cabinet were dumped into the sink. My mother refused to let Keegan call the police.

"I don't want the cops here," Mom said. "It'll draw more attention than it's worth. Besides, it looks like they found what they were looking for." I suspected our mother knew who had been in our home, and what they stole, but she didn't tell me. I was scared going to sleep that night, and Keegan pushed the couch up against the front door. Since then he's installed new locks on all of the doors and the windows. I never talked about it to anyone, not even David.

David. His round face and dark blue eyes flash through my mind. I wonder how angry he was when he got back to the truck and discovered that I had left.

Will this be the end of our relationship? He's gorgeous, and funny, and charms all the teachers. A good student, not straight As, but still above average. He's not a loner like some guys; he has a group of friends, and he invites my friends to tag along with us to the movies. And he can fix anything. He even works on Mom's car for free and gave Keegan advice on what type of used car to buy. And he goes to church with his mom, not every week, but at least once a month. I admire David for his strong beliefs. My family never goes to church. I wonder about it sometimes.

The times we struggle, where it isn't as easy, are his ways to tell wrong from right. He's got these hard and fast lines. One of them is being gay, or queer, or anything like that. It isn't a big deal to me if someone is that way. I'm not gay, but I don't care if someone else is. That's just who they are. Sure, I feel a little uncomfortable when someone is openly kissing another person of the same sex, but mostly it's uncomfortable because everyone around is reacting to it. Why can't two girls or two guys just start kissing in the hallway without half the student body freaking out? Even most of the teachers let it slide. As long as hands are appropriately placed around the shoulders, then the lips can be glued together. David, though, always gets angry. He says it's against God, written in the Bible, that sex is about procreation, between a man and a woman. I've never read the Bible, but David claims it's in there.

God may condemn homosexuality, but I'm pretty sure God wouldn't condone what David and MJ did to Ricky and Jonathan. Jonathan and Ricky, naked and kissing. I've never seen anything like it. It was surreal and kind of shocking, too, if I think about it from David's perspective. For someone like David, it must have been a shock. I grab a sweater out of my closet and see my sparkling blue prom dress hanging ready for this weekend. I lay my hand on it for just a moment. Then I move to the breakfast table. I kind of understand what happened, why things got out of hand.

My mom is moving around the kitchen, making lunches and stopping to read the Mountain Express on her iPad. She's a tall, slender woman with a silver mane braided down her back. She looks tired. The wrinkles above her eyebrows are always deeper when she isn't sleeping much.

"Sorry I got in late last night," she admits, and looks up at me. "Did I see your light on when I pulled in?" I wonder if she knows it was Keegan who brought me home instead of David.

"I didn't hear you come in or I would have said goodnight, Mom," I lie, keeping my voice steady. My squirming intestines are threatening to send me back to the bathroom. "Will you have to be out again this week?" I ask. It would be nice to have her home.

Mom is searching the local news and ignores my question. She stops and taps the iPad, looking worried.

"What's this? 'Local Boy Beaten Up: Gay Bashing in Mount Lincoln'? Did you hear about this, Leda?"

"Let me see that." I pull the iPad towards me. There's a picture of Ricky, and it looks like a school photo; he's wearing a brown plaid shirt that matches his eyes, and his lemon locks are pushed to the side. His eyes smile. He looks like he's holding in a secret and bursting to share it with someone. I feel heat rise up, flushing my cheeks, as I read the report. He was taken away by ambulance, laid out on a stretcher. They call him a victim. Threads of vomit make their way up my throat, and the kitchen walls start to close in. The appliances are growing and sucking the air out of the room.

I take a deep breath. "I need to finish getting ready for school," I whisper, and start to walk back towards my bedroom.

"Wait," Mom cries, grabbing my arm. "Do you know this kid?"

"Yeah, he's my science lab partner."

"Oh, Leda, I'm sorry, you must be worried sick."

"Yeah. I just want to get to school so I can find out what happened," I say, and she releases my arm.

"Any other news in there?" I ask, trying to be supportive, knowing that she's also worried about herself. She doesn't sell that much, but she's likely the one that would take the fall. Her day job, caretaking for older people who are housebound, pays minimum wage. When my dad passed away, there wasn't very much payout by the insurance. They said black ice is a natural event, not something they could control. She got just enough to keep us from losing the house. But all other expenses landed on her, and one day some guy at the temp agency asked if she wanted to make some money on the side. All she had to do was pocket one or two pills a day from each of the patients she cares for. She's already in the homes; she already picks up their meds for them. It's easy, and the old people have no clue. Half the time they get more drugs prescribed to them than they know what to do with, so it's not really hurting anyone. She's said to us lots of times, "It's just so I can pay the bills. Once I'm caught up, I'll stop." But it's been three years.

"Nope, all's quiet on the Eastern Front." She smiles at me.

When Keegan pulls the car up Friday morning to drop me off, the entire student body seems to be hanging out in the courtyard as if it's the end of the day. Our car is the focus of conversation, and heads huddle up to whisper. They're waiting to see who steps out, like a red carpet. Two state police cars are parked in the fire lanes and the officers stand in front of the school talking to Principal Rafferty.

"Shit. Looks like the school is going to be involved," Keegan says. My phone starts to buzz and David's face appears on the screen.

"David?" I answer.

"Hey, Leda. Where did you go last night? You took off before the fun was over." His voice is all business.

"I caught a ride home with Keegan," I reply, looking up at my brother for reassurance.

"Are you at school yet?" he asks.

"Yeah. Where are you?" I'm not even sure if I want to see him.

"I'm at home, called in sick. Too much happening."

My stomach plunges to my knees. Maybe I'm sick too. David rushes on.

"If any cops start asking you questions, you know what to say, right? You're my alibi, Leda. I told my folks that you and I were together all night. I dropped you off at home around midnight. So you have to back me up, okay?"

"Wait, what do you mean? Why would the cops be asking me anything?" I say.

"Well, you know, because those queers, they're such victims, they might think it was me and MJ. I don't know. It was dark, so I don't think they could really see us, but if they do try to pin this on us—listen, I can't take the fall for this. I thought we were just going to scare them a little. I told you I wasn't going to hurt anyone. I told MJ we had to get out of there. I got him to stop, but if I get charged with this thing, it will ruin my chances of getting a scholarship to play ball. You know that's the only way I'm going to get to college. I don't have the grades, or the money."

I feel sick. "So, where were we supposed to be?" I ask. Keegan rolls his eyes at me and opens his mouth to protest, but I shush him with my finger.

"I told them we were on Tully Hill." That makes sense. Tully Hill is off the beaten path. It's where people go to mess around. It's one of our secret spots, and it's usually empty on a weeknight.

"I can't believe this is happening," I say. "I have to go, David."

"But you'll back me up, right?" His voice is confident.

"Yeah. What else am I supposed to do?" It's true.

"I love you, Leda." I don't respond, but I feel my head nodding at the phone.

I hang up and look at Keegan.

"He wants you to cover for him."

"Yes . . . Why? You wouldn't?" I secretly want to be told what to do. Keegan's never been much for advice, but there's always a first time.

"Jesus, I don't know either. How's getting involved going to help?" Keegan asks.

"But I am involved. I was with him at Charlie's Pizza after work and he told his parents already that I was with him all night, that we were on Tully Hill. Keegan, I don't want him to go to jail. He's not a bad person. It'll fuck up his whole life. Plus, he knows about Mom. If I turn him in—"

"Great, that's just what we need."

"I know, but what am I supposed to do?"

Keegan shrugs, but doesn't offer any more words of wisdom. That's just the way he rolls. He had his fun in high school, screwed around, smoked too much weed and almost flunked out. But now he's just try-ing to stay focused on getting some intro classes under his belt at the community college so he can get into the University of Vermont. He's decided to become an architect like Dad, and he's getting back on track. Like a switch flipped and suddenly he isn't my loser brother anymore: he has Goals. And he's pushed me to think about college too.

"I gotta get to work, Leda. But hang in there, okay?"

"Sure. Thanks for the ride," I mumble as I climb out of the car and move towards the school entrance.

A female officer with long, black hair down her back is talking to Principal Rafferty. As I approach the build-ing, I think I hear my name.

"I'd really prefer that you only speak to the students with their parents' permission," Principal Rafferty says, looking strained.

"Sure, sure," the officer nods, all the while jotting

down notes on a small pad of paper. I keep moving. The gray tile floor seems uneven beneath my feet.

Kira runs up to me. "Oh my god, did you hear what happened to Ricky?" Kira is also in chemistry with us, and sometimes she does labs with us when her partner is absent. She's not the brightest crayon in the box, and she always falls all over the cute guys, but she's friendly. I like her. If it weren't for the small patches of psoriasis that creep across her neck and cheeks, she would be pretty.

"What?" I try to sound appropriately concerned and clueless.

"Someone beat him and Jonathan up at the reservoir last night. Can you believe it? Ricky is in the hospital, apparently in a catatonic state, with broken ribs and a gashed face."

This time my horror is real, and I can tell Kira is excited to be the one to share the news with me. She furrows her dark brows, but all the while her cheeks are slanted upwards, caught in a secret smile. That's the way it is in a small town; a terrible crime isn't just news, it's gossip. This story will be teased apart from every angle by every person, because there literally is nothing else to talk about.

"What about Jonathan?" I ask, unsure if I want to hear the answer.

"I guess he's home with his mom," Kira reports. "Apparently he swam away and didn't get seriously hurt. They took a few pellets out of his leg, but he had to watch while they beat up Ricky. Pretty awful, huh?"

"Yeah." It is awful. "Do the police know who did it?"

Kira shakes her head. "No, it could have been anyone. I mean, there are lots people in this town who hate queers."

"Don't use that word, Kira."

"Why not? They call themselves queer."

"I know, but I think it's like the N-word for black people. You can only use it if you are one."

"Sorry. I mean gays." She looks at me sheepishly, her curly bangs sliding over her eyes. "Are you going to go see Ricky at the hospital?"

"I don't know," I reply honestly, thinking about Ricky's reaction to my presence. Jonathan won't want me there. He only associates me with David.

The first bell rings and I move towards history. Everyone in class is buzzing about Ricky and Jonathan. Abbey Riggs, a classic cheerleader, scooches to the end of her seat just behind me.

"Hey Leda, where's David today? Doesn't he usually walk you to class?"

"He's home, sick," I report, giving my best no-big-deal face. But I see Abbey lean back to her best friend, Hannah, and whisper something. They both turn and look at me with worried expressions. Sometimes it feels like they only tolerate my presence in their lives because I'm David's girlfriend.

"Tell him we hope he feels better. Wouldn't want to miss prom," Abbey says, just as the teacher clears his throat and calls for us to settle down.

Prom on Saturday, I'd actually almost forgotten. It was amazing to be in the spotlight, something David is used to, but not me. He took his place in the starting lineup for the game and unrolled a poster asking me to prom, and everyone cheered when I said yes. I have a sparkly blue dress that matches my eyes and fancy heels and David rented a gray tux. I can't wait to see him in it. He says I'm the only girl he would ever dress in a monkey suit for.

By noon I'm sitting in Latin Three. That's when Mrs. Rafferty shows up and hands a note to my teacher, who looks directly at me. I lower my eyes to the conjugated verbs on my paper, but before I know it I'm following Mrs. Rafferty down the hallway and being led into the principal's glass-framed office. I don't know what I'm going to say.

The officer waiting for me is the same woman I saw earlier this morning. And there is my mom, looking distraught. Her long braid is no longer tightly woven; instead she looks as though she rubbed her head with a balloon. When I walk over to the seat next to her, she leaps to her feet, as if prepared to grab me by the arm and drag me out of there.

Instead, my mother is actually trying to be reassuring. "Honey, Officer Templeton has a few questions to ask you about where you were last night." She looks me in the eye, "You are not in any trouble—"

The officer cuts her off. "Thank you, Mrs. Keogh, but I think it's important not to make any promises." Then she turns to me.

"Hello, Miss Keogh. Your mom's right, I do have a few questions for you. Do you mind taking a seat next to your mom?" I nod and sit down. My mouth sticks together like a huge wad of dry Kleenex.

"Can you tell me what you did after school and into the evening of Thursday, May eighteenth?"

I take a breath. "I took the bus home after school, finished up my homework, had some dinner with my mom, and watched old *Friends* episodes until about seven thirty."

"What did you have for dinner?"

"What? Why does it matter what I had for dinner?"

"Just answer the question, please."

"Chicken, rice, and peas."

"What happened at seven thirty?" The officer is taking notes on a thin pad of paper.

"I walked to Slayton's Auto Body to meet up with my boyfriend."

"And your boyfriend's name?"

"David Slayton. His dad owns the shop. He works for him after school until the shop closes."

"Where did you and Mr. Slayton go?" the officer asks. I hesitate, but look around at my mother and realize she wants to hear this just as badly as the cop.

"Around," I reply. This isn't good.

"Around where, Leda? Can you tell the officer where?" my mom interjects, and I glare at her.

"We drove around. We stopped back at his dad's garage because he forgot something, and then we went over to Charlie's Pizza Pub and had a pizza. David hadn't eaten yet. I had a milkshake."

"What did he forget?" Officer Templeton asks.

"Um, money, he needed money to go get pizza," I state, as if it should be obvious. Why aren't they asking David these questions?

"Do you remember what flavor?"

46

"What?"

"I need to know the details of your evening with Mr. Slayton," she encourages me with a nod.

"I had a chocolate milkshake, large," I state. I've watched cops on TV and this is nothing that interesting. These questions are kind of stupid.

"Where did you go when you left Charlie's Pizza Pub?" Officer Templeton's voice is steady.

"We drove around, looking for a place to hang out, and went to Tully Hill."

"Oh good lord." My mother can barely contain herself.

"Tully Hill?" The officer is feigning stupidity. Surely, she knows what it is. She just wants me to say it out loud.

"Yeah, you know . . . Lover's Lane, whatever you want to call it." I can't help but smirk a little. This is ridiculous.

"And then what happened?"

"We hung out."

"What time did you arrive at Tully Hill?"

"About nine thirty, maybe ten."

"What time did Mr. Slayton drive you home?"

"You make it sound like I was with David's dad. He's a kid."

"Well, not exactly, Leda. He's eighteen; legally he's an adult. But if you prefer, I'll call him David. What time did David bring you home?"

"About midnight, I guess." I glance at Mom, who is calculating in her head how long we were parked on Tully Hill.

"And what were you and Mr.—ah, I'm sorry, what were you and David doing in his truck on Tully Hill?"

I can feel the pressure of my eyes bulging. What does she think I'm going to do, give her every detail of every minute David and I spent together, right there in front of my mother? I go the innocent route and smile shakily: "I'm not sure I know what you want me to describe?"

"Please, Leda. Can you tell me what you did on Tully Hill for approximately two to two and a half hours?"

Damn. "We talked." I exaggerate the word to make the point that I do not wish to continue this part of the conversation.

"What did you talk about?" Officer Templeton doesn't flinch.

"I don't know, nothing, everything—we'd had a fight earlier in the week and we were making up."

"What did you fight about?" Officer Templeton's eyes pierce me and I look away. *Oh shit.*

My mom breaks in. "Honestly, Officer, I'm not sure how that would be helpful evidence. They're kids. They fight all the time, like all relationships."

The officer glares at my mother. She turns back to me and I give her a weak smile.

"It's getting close to the end of the school year," I say, "David is ready to go off to college and I have another year to go. We were fighting about whether or not we can stay together. I said we can't, that David should be single going to college, but he says he'll wait for me. I'm hoping to get into an art program where he's going for baseball."

I tear up a little, because I wish this was what we were fighting about. David doesn't have the slightest interest in staying together after he graduates, except maybe through the summer. He's made it clear he wants to be a free agent. He cares and all, but he's going to LA, and as he likes to remind me, there are a lot of pretty women in LA.

"I see. And is David the only person who can confirm your story?"

"What?" My mother jumps in again, coming undone. "Are you calling my daughter a liar?"

"Mrs. Keogh, please calm down. There is a young man lying in a hospital with a broken nose and cracked ribs and other internal injuries. He may never be the same again, and his friend named your daughter's boyfriend as someone who might have done it. Now, I have a job to do: to understand what happened last night. Everything your daughter tells me is evidence. If David is responsible for this, then he needs to be held accountable. On the other hand, if he wasn't there, then I need to know that so we can clear his name. We don't put eighteen-year-olds behind bars on a whim, okay?"

Mom settles back into her seat, clutches her bag close to her chest, and gives me an anxious look. I just shake my head.

"What is David's relationship with Ricky Norton?" asks Officer Templeton, redirecting the conversation back to me.

I think about this, remembering our fight. *Did you study fairy dust today in chemistry, Leda? I see a fairy escaped the lab. This freakin' school is full of fairies. A few people around us laughed, and I could see Ricky's shoulders droop and his head tip forward. Where's your boyfriend? Did you forget your fairy queen? Red splotches formed on the back of Ricky's neck. With my arm still looped in David's I dragged my feet, giving him a few paces to escape. Then David took a big step forward and pulled Ricky's book down from his arms, sending the notes we had just spent an hour working on flying through the hallway.*

Leave him alone, David!

Go fuck yourself, Leda.

It took two days of text flirting to get him to forgive me. Then I got the idea to go swimming after he got off from work at his father's garage. Even though it was a school night, I just wanted us to make up before the weekend.

I hear myself answer. "David doesn't really have a relationship with Ricky. I don't even know if he knows who Ricky is."

"In a small school of only three hundred students, and seventy-five seniors, David doesn't know him? Doesn't know the boy who is your lab partner?"

I'm surprised she knows Ricky is my lab partner.

"I'm not saying he doesn't know who Ricky is, but they hang out in different crowds, you know? Just because we all go to the same school doesn't mean we're all best friends."

"Okay. I'll ask in a different way. What kind of inter-actions have you noticed between David and Ricky in school?"

I don't want to do this anymore. "I haven't noticed any interactions. I don't think they really talk to each other." The officer is writing lots of notes and keeps flipping pages. I want to tell her to get an iPad or something. I look over to my mom, who is biting her lip. It looks like it's about to start bleeding.

"What about between MJ and Ricky?"

"MJ?" I ask, and suck in my breath. "Why would I know anything about MJ?"

"Isn't MJ David's best friend?" Officer Templeton asks.

"Yeah. I mean, they're good friends. David has other friends too," I say, hoping this will steer them towards other possible suspects.

"Do you spend time with David and MJ together?"

"I guess. Sometimes."

"Well, have you ever noticed any interactions between MJ and Ricky?"

"No." Another nail in my coffin of lies. Officer Templeton looks at me for a long, silent minute. "Are we done yet? I really need to get back to class."

She looks over her notes, and then pulls a business card out of her front left pocket. She hands the card to me and then stands to go. She shakes my mother's hand. "Thank you for your time, Mrs. Keogh, feel free to call me if your daughter has any further information to share."

Then she turns to me. "I don't know exactly what happened last night, Leda, but I hope Ricky's friends don't let him down." She stares me square in my guilt-filled eyes. I give up and shift my gaze to the floor, waiting like an animal to be released from a snare.

I walk Mom to the front door of the school so she can go back to work. She hesitates, and I think she's going to give me a hug. "What?" I ask.

"Are you going home right after school?"

"Yeah, I guess, why?"

"I'm having a friend over after work." Her voice lilts on the word friend, so I know it's the guy she sells to.

"Why is he coming to the house?" I ask, despite my reluctance to hear the answer.

She doesn't want to hug me, she's angry. "Because we were going to meet earlier, but I had to go talk to the cops with you. I told him about it. I think he just wants to assess the situation."

"That's none of his business, Mom."

She stares back at me.

"Fine. I'll go to the library." I barely look at her. "I have to get to class."

"Okay, it shouldn't take long, but that's a good idea," she says, looking relieved. She turns away and heads out the door, checking her watch.

I make my way back towards class, passing the principal's office once more. The police officer is gone and instead I notice a tall, thin woman with curly hair speaking with Mrs. Rafferty and Mrs. Goodrich, the guidance counselor. There is something familiar about her, but I can't place it. She is noticeably upset. I move quietly down the hallway. On the wall is a bulletin board with summer job postings. Most of them are minimum wage jobs at places like the Whippy Dip and the farmers market. Jobs that end with the summer. The jobs that pay more go to friends or kids of friends and never get posted on anyone's bulletin board. I remember seeing the principal's daughter working at the General Store, heard her bragging about how her dad is in the same bowling league as the owner, and that's how she landed such a cushy job.

One flyer stands out. It has a picture of a red canoe bobbing on a lake, and it reads: "Spend the summer on a lake and get paid. Wanted: full-time nanny for a seven-year-old girl. Must be a young woman, sixteen or over, who is willing to play make-believe games for large parts of the day, is a proficient swimmer, and has boating skills."

I unpin the flyer, fold it neatly into a square that will fit into the front pocket of my jeans, and head down the hallway. Through the window, I see the same woman getting into her car. All of a sudden I recognize her as Jonathan's mother. Opening night of the school play she was in front row seats with someone, must have been Jonathan's dad. I study her face for a moment. She looks pissed and frustrated as hell. I fight an urge to run to her and blurt out the whole story. She looks up, peering at the school as if she can see me. My legs stiffen. I turn and head down the hall in the opposite direction, desperate to get back to class where everything is normal.

6

✦

Jonathan Tanner-Eales

A BAD EXCUSE

THE BRUISES on Ricky's body are shifting from deep purples to greens and yellows, like when algae surfaces on the lake and the water reflects the sky. It's amazing to watch his body heal itself. I carve these colors into my memory, these colors, the patterns of bruises on Ricky's perpetually tanned skin.

Five days, seven hours, and forty-three minutes have passed since Ricky was brought to the hospital. I watch him breathe. I take turns with Mr. and Mrs. Norton. We hold vigil over our sleeping boy, who moves around as if dreaming, but never opens his eyes. At first Mrs. Norton tried to send me away, but I pleaded to stay and Mr. Norton came to my defense. He said that his son wouldn't even be alive if it weren't for me.

Not true, I think. *He wouldn't be catatonic if it wasn't for me.*

After hours of tests and images, it was determined that Ricky has four broken ribs, a broken nose, and a fractured collarbone. He had internal bleeding from tears in his stomach, and one kidney was damaged so severely it had to be removed. There were blows to his face, but no fractures in his skull. Within twenty-four hours he was stitched up, taped up, and drugged up.

The doctors tell us daily that his body is healing remarkably well. And each day, I am hopeful that Ricky will wake up. The best explanation the doctors can give us is that Ricky went into shock. They believe it happened fairly quickly, that he may not have even felt the beating.

"His mind is protecting itself," explains one young physician, who claims to be specializing in psychological trauma. "Catatonic is a state of neurogenic motor immobility that can be induced by Post-Traumatic Stress Disorder." The Nortons lean closer to their son, as if they can protect him from the words bouncing off the sterile walls.

"Isn't post trauma—PT, whatever you call it—something veterans get after they've been to war?" Mrs. Norton asks.

"PTSD, yes. It can occur in people who serve in a war, but it can be caused by any traumatic situation. Not everyone who suffers from PTSD goes into a catatonic state, but it is not out of the realm of possibility."

"Can't you treat it?" I ask. The doctor looks down at Ricky's chart and then back to his bed.

"Yes, once we've given him time to come out of it himself. It's better for his recovery if he's able to bring himself back to reality without medication. The most important thing we can do at this point is to help him feel safe, talk with him, reassure him that he is with family and friends. Once his body has recovered enough, if he remains in this state, we'll have to move him to the psychiatric ward. But for now, while we're still monitoring his physical wounds, we'll keep him here."

I return home each evening from the hospital feeling totally depleted. I read articles online about PTSD, trying to understand the science behind it. That's what Ricky would do. He's such a nerd; he would be fascinated by the connection between physical and psychological trauma. I save each article. I'll share them with Ricky once he's better.

I do my best to avoid Mom. Most days this is easily accomplished. She's stopped by the hospital to see Ricky and talk with Mr. and Mrs. Norton, but I suspect she's actually checking up on me. Today she's lurking near the kitchen, anticipating my exit.

"Where are you headed?" she asks. As if she doesn't already know the answer.

"To the hospital," I reply.

"Did you talk with your teachers about wrapping up your classwork and taking final exams, like we discussed?" she prods carefully, leaning up against the kitchen island, bracing herself for my pushback. I don't want to think about school and the asshole rednecks that go there. I told Officer Templeton I thought it was David and MJ who attacked us, but how could I be sure? I heard that Leda is David's alibi—that he was with her the whole evening up on Tully Hill. I think they're lying. Thinking about this is infuriating. How could she? Ricky always spoke highly of Leda, called her his friend. I never really trusted her. She's David's girlfriend, after all.

"I sent them emails. They don't expect me back in their classes, and they don't care if I finish my school-work. My grades are fine as is. I'm not going to fail."

"And you're okay with that?"

"Jesus, Mom, I'm not stepping back into that school. I told you I'm pretty sure the guys who did this to Ricky are there—every day they're there, and I'm not . . . it's not—" My words falter. Their words still echo in my ear: *If we catch you . . .*

"I'm not asking you to go back to the school when they're in the building. It's just that you have as much right to finish your school year as they do, whoever they are."

"I know! Do you think I don't know that?" I turn to face the door. I'm done with this conversation. I'm done with this town. "I'm not going back there, Mom."

"Hold on, Jonathan. What do you mean? That you're not going back there today—or ever?"

"I'm not going back to that school, ever. It's a cess-pool of ignorant hicks."

"Honey, the people who did this are terrible human beings. They don't represent the town."

I turn back to her, so angry that she can think this. "You have no idea, Mom. They aren't the only ones. There are plenty of kids who barely tolerate me and Ricky and treat us like shit. This isn't Eden, Mom, every-one and their asshole dad has a pickup truck and thinks gays are gross." I'm having a hard time breathing.

"What? Why haven't you said this before?" she asks. I drop my head. I want to dismantle the wall I built to protect her with a pick ax.

"It sucks going to this school, Mom. I wanted to tell you, but you were so happy to be away from Dad, and I figured I could handle it."

"Handle what?" she demands.

"The guys at the school. They're assholes, most of them. They act like they own the place."

"Have they hurt you before, Jonathan? Have they hurt Ricky?" she whispers. I wipe my forehead. The memories of the past year line up like dominoes.

"They pull all kinds of shit, Mom. Like blocking doors so we can't get in or out, and catcalling Ricky. They call us faggots and fairies. They like to pick on Ricky more than me, because I'm bigger. But Ricky doesn't have the same confidence. He's more," I hesitate, thinking of the right word, "fragile."

My mother's whole body has stiffened up. Her face is incredulous, but she takes me by the arm and leads me to the couch as if we can sort this out. "Where are the teachers when all of this is happening? I don't understand. How they could let this go on? Have you ever told your teachers?" She's in search of the climate control she believes exists in the hallways of schools.

"I've tried to tell the music teacher, Mr. Fuller, but he just kind of nods, like he gets how tough it is. He hasn't had any suggestions . . . Well, once he told me I could file a complaint to the principal, but then he reminded me that the principal's husband is the football coach. I think he was warning me I wouldn't get much support there." My eyes stay fixed on the floor. I feel uncomfortable admitting my failure at handling this.

"The school should have been protecting you," she declares. The lines on her forehead deepen, and her hands curl into fists, ready to jump into the ring. "I should have been protecting you! I had no idea you and Ricky were putting up with this kind of abuse. I thought you would be safe here."

"It's not your fault, Mom. Maybe there are places in the state that are better, but Mount Lincoln isn't one of them. Most of the families have lived here forever, and they think that men are men because they have sex with women." Now that I've started I can't stop. "They believe God is an old white guy in the clouds! Anyone who doesn't fit their idea of what a manly man is or does is wrong. And they get uncomfortable and mad when someone challenges them. It's just how they are."

Mom looks at me for a long time before pulling me into a hug. I lean my head down, resting it on her shoulder. "Maybe we should get out of town," she suggests.

I pull away from her. "I can't leave Ricky," I say, because I can't. "Not now."

I pull into the parking lot of the hospital blaring the Arctic Monkeys. The noise fills me up and calms me. My head rests against the steering wheel, eyes closed, and then someone raps on my window. I jump a little and refocus to see Anita, Ricky's younger sister, standing next to my car. I haven't seen her at the hospital before.

"Hey, I thought that was you. Are you going in?" she asks. I nod, climb out of the car, and we make our way to Ricky's room.

When we get there, Anita flops into the green plastic chair near the window. Her platinum-blonde locks are pulled tight into a ponytail. Her hands are tucked into the pockets of her sweatshirt. "Has he talked yet?" Anita asks, as she avoids letting her gaze land on Ricky.

I take a deep breath. "Why don't you ask him?" I say this half under my breath. Anita looks from me to him, assessing the situation, and her knee pumps jerkily up and down.

"Well, it looks to me like he's sleeping. I can come back another day." She gets up to leave, but I stand up too.

"Where are you going?" I ask. "You just got here. Why do you need to rush off?" She looks me over, weighing her options.

"Why do you care? He's just lying there like a freak—as if his life wasn't screwed up enough, now he's a vegetable."

"Don't say that. It's not true. If you spent a little time with him, you'd know he's going to be okay. He's going to pull out of this. You have to talk to him, reassure him he's safe, like the doctors said." My cheeks flush with frustration. "And what do you mean, his life is screwed up?"

I know she's referring to Ricky being gay, but I don't feel like letting it go. That's what I always do: I let the digs go, the attitude, the snarky remarks. How often does Ricky's sexuality inconvenience his sister?

60

"Look, Jonathan. I'm not here to thank you for saving my brother, or not saving him." She looks up at me quickly. "Or whatever."

"Really?" I counter. "Do you think I called those guys and asked them to come to the reservoir to beat up your brother? Oh, I'm sorry, is your popularity being affected by it?" I want her to take back her words.

"Leave me alone, Jonathan. I don't have to talk to you about this."

She's right. I nod at her, and sit back down. "You're right. You don't."

She stalks past me and I let her go, feeling defeated. I pull the chair closer to Ricky's bedside and rub his forearm. Ricky thought it was best to come out to them all together, so he waited until Thanksgiving dinner and offered to say grace before the meal. The way Ricky explained it to me, he knew his father would be upset, but he was sure his sister would stand up for him, like she always had. So when Ricky said the blessing, he added at the end, "And thank you to my loving family for supporting me for being gay." Anita was silent for a moment. Then she stood up and whispered, "Oh my god, why are you doing this?" and then left. Apparently everyone sat around not talking until Ricky's parents just went ahead and started eating. No one talked about it again. When I first met the family, they all treated me as if I was the virus their son had caught. I look down at Ricky and say a prayer. Not a prayer to God, or Allah, or some deity specifically, I just say the same four words over and over in my head: Please make him okay. Please make him okay. Please make him okay.

Later that afternoon, Mrs. Norton arrives at the hospital, ready to relieve me. She works the seven-to-three shifts at Mac's Deli five days a week, and these are the hours I try to be with Ricky. It isn't that Mrs. Norton doesn't like me, not like before, it's just that we never know what to say to each other. When she first enters the room, Ricky turns away from us onto his side, his face towards the wall. It's weird. His eyes stay closed, but he moves around a lot.

"Hey," I mumble, nodding to Mrs. Norton.

"Hey, yourself," she replies. Her blond, curly hair is wrapped tightly into a bun on her head. She's still wearing a hair net.

"Did something happen?" I ask, wondering if she hurried out of work.

"No, I just came from work. Why?"

I point at her head, and her hand rushes to her bun. She smiles and pulls the netting off with a blush, stuffing it into the pocket of her jeans. "Sometimes I get so lost in thought . . ." she explains, but quickly falls silent and I lower my eyes.

"I think about it all the time too," I offer. I'm feeling brave after arguing with Anita.

"What do you think about?" she asks.

"That day, what happened, what I could have done differently . . ." I trail off.

Words pour from her mouth. "Do you ever think about before that day? What led up to that day? Did you ever wonder if it was safe to be off by yourselves? When you knew Ricky was being bullied by those assholes at school?"

I'm stunned at the accusation in her voice. She thinks

it's my fault. There's a crack of anger she's barely holding in. Did Anita tell her about our argument?

"No. I mean, I knew, but I didn't think . . ."

"That's right," she retorts. "You didn't think about anything but your own libidos." Her voice is rising and a red flush is moving up her neck. "You . . . for months, Ricky has shown up at home with bruises from being punched in the arm. Or tripped in the hallway. His notebook covers have crude drawings on them. Horrible drawings! And slurs written by idiots who think they're funny."

She raises her right arm in front of her and yanks her sleeve down towards her elbow. "I wondered why he was using up so many notebooks. Until I found them under his bed. I told his father months ago that we should talk with the principal about the way he was being treated, but he said Ricky needed to learn to fight his own battles. But you!" Her tone rises higher. "You knew what was happening! Why didn't you help him? Why did you take him off to a secluded place where he could be attacked?"

She grabs her mouth to stop herself from yelling more, and the tears stream from the slits of her closed eyes. I stare at her anguished face, feeling remorse for all of it, and remember the many times I saw the bruises on Ricky's arms, the cut on his lip after being pushed up the stairs by a group of football players who treated him worse than pigskin. Ricky didn't fight back because he didn't stand a chance against them. And he was afraid.

I'm furious and my eyes feel hot. I stand up. "I never left him alone on purpose, Mrs. Norton. I met him after class whenever I could, and walked him to the next one, even if I was going to be late for mine. I knew I had to protect him."

"And yet, you still went to the reservoir to swim, at night, with no one around." Her mouth contorts as she tries not to cry harder. The accusation hangs between us. Her eyes cut into me.

"Stop it!"

A voice from the bed. Mrs. Norton and I turn to look at Ricky, whose eyes are wide open. He's awake. He looks pissed and confused. Relief and joy wash over me. It doesn't matter anymore that Mrs. Norton is angry or that I failed, because he's awake. I step closer to the bed, and Mrs. Norton does too.

"You talked," Mrs. Norton whispers. "Ricky?" She reaches out to him.

"Yes. And I can hear too. You can't blame Jonathan, Mom."

I look into Ricky's eyes. We stare at each other. I wonder what he remembers.

"You're here because I couldn't protect you, Ricky," I whisper, and my voice breaks.

The nurses call button finally produces a short ginger-haired woman who is all smiles when she hears Ricky ask for water with ice. The three of us spend the rest of the afternoon talking quietly. Mrs. Norton dotes on Ricky, watching his every movement, and fills him in on the events of the last week. She even shows him pictures of his sister's prom dress, and Ricky seems genuinely interested. We avoid the topic of that night at the reservoir, not wanting to upset him. Alan and Anita arrive at the hospital shortly before dinner. Anita ignores me and hugs her brother close. Maybe all is forgiven. I take this as a sign I should head home and give them some time together.

"Stay a moment," Mrs. Norton commands. "We'll go grab something from the café and be back." They leave the room, allowing me a few moments with Ricky alone.

I touch his hand. "I'm glad you're talking again," I say, giving him a small grin and searching his face for the softness between us. Ricky's blond hair is long and straggly. His bruises are muted now, but still yellow and brown. He looks around the room before meeting my eyes. Something is wrong.

"Jonathan," he says slowly, "I think you should not visit for a while."

Everything gets a little fuzzy. "What?"

He gathers speed. "I need some time. Looking at you . . . it brings it all back." His words disappear into sterile linens. Silence fills the room. I don't know how to respond. He starts to apologize.

"I'm sorry, Jonathan, it's just . . ." he whispers. But this time I can do the right thing.

"I get it," I say, beating him to it. He doesn't owe me anything. If anything, it's the other way around. I owe him whatever he asks for.

"You've been here every day?" he asks. I just nod. I can't really talk. Tears are streaming down my face.

"Well, jeez man, take a break." He smiles emptily like a TV host. "It's summer. Go do something fun. Just give me a little time." He looks up at me. There's panic around the edges of his eyes.

I nod and smile the best I can. I squeeze his hand and bend over to kiss his forehead. But he turns towards the wall and my lips graze the side of his head.

I love him.

"I love you," I whisper. Ricky keeps his eyes focused on the wall as I stand and walk out the door.

7

✦

Leda Keogh

DENIAL

"I DID WHAT you wanted David, I backed you up!"
We're in the hallway of the Elks Lodge. David picked
me up for the prom at seven. We didn't eat out with
friends like we were planning, but David's father told
him not to avoid his normal activities because it just
makes him look as if he's hiding something. I didn't
really want to go anymore, but David insisted. And ever
since I climbed into his truck, he's been grilling me on
my meeting with the police.

"You must have let something slip, Leda. Why else
would they show up at my house?"

David's hand is squeezing my wrist, pulling me down
the corridor and away from chaperoning ears. He looks
over his shoulder for people meandering their way
to the restrooms. He lowers his voice even more and
pushes me behind a huge glass trophy case.

"I told them we were at Tully Hill, just like you said. They spoke to lots of people at school, David. Maybe someone saw us on the way to the reservoir?" David thinks about this and loosens his grip. Worry lines stretch across his forehead.

"The cop said she was doing everything she could to clear your name," I add. David looks surprised and almost relieved.

"Yeah? Well, they better clear my name. I'm not taking the hit for MJ. He did most of it." He looks like a small child. I hope MJ takes the blame to keep David safe. I take a deep breath and pull him into a hug. His aftershave wafts over us and he wraps his arms around me. I feel him relax.

"Break it up, you two!" Mr. Simmons says, walking towards us. "Go on back into the dance, the hallways are off-limits."

We make our way back to the dance floor where Abbey, Kira, and a few others are dancing with their dates. Dancing is my least favorite part of dances, but I let David pull my hips towards his and we move together. He's warm and solid.

When the song ends, Kira grabs my elbow and leads me to the refreshment table. David nods his approval, falling back to hang with the boys. "You and David look so sweet together," Kira says, leaning her face close to mine so I can hear her above the music. "I was surprised to see him here."

"What do you mean?" I ask.

"Well, it's just that everyone says . . ." Her voice trails off and I can see that she wants me to confirm the rumor.

"Everyone says what?" I demand. Kira just looks at me, embarrassed. I keep on the offensive. "For your information, Kira, David was with me that night, on Tully Hill. He wasn't anywhere near the reservoir." I grab a cup of soda and drink it down, then throw it in the trash and turn away from her. Kira puts her hand on my shoulder to slow my departure.

"I'm sorry, Leda!" she cries. "I didn't mean to spread more rumors. I didn't know that you were together. Of course you were together, why didn't I think of that?" Kira is rushing to keep up with me.

"Who told you to ask me about David?" I ask, slowing our pace back to the circle. I can see Abbey and Hannah watching us closely. Maybe Kira's just a pawn. Apparently they don't have the guts to ask me themselves.

"No one!" Kira says quickly. "I didn't mean to offend you, Leda."

"No worries," I say, leaving her standing alone. I walk back to David and lead him to the dance floor. No one else mentions Ricky or Jonathan for the rest of the night.

A few days later, to avoid my chemistry homework, I reach for my sketchpad, and beneath it I find that job posting for being a nanny. I told David about it, hoping he would be excited, but he really wants me to stay in Mount Lincoln. I think he's scared of what might happen since the police are still asking questions. He won't say that, but I can hear it in his voice. Keegan actually found the flyer on my desk and keeps asking me if I've called yet. It's sweet. Ever since I called him last week to pick me up, he comes into my room just to talk and check in, especially when I'm painting. He busies him-self squeezing the paint towards the cap of the tube so I can get it out easier.

"You should call them, Leda. It could be good for you to just get out of town for a while." So I make the call. And leave an awkward message.

A Mrs. Woodruff calls me back, and she invites me to meet her and Maddie, her seven-year-old daughter, on Friday after school. The Woodruffs must be rich. They live outside of town on a multi-acre estate. Their pri-vate road weaves through a young birch forest and leads to their modern-looking house. There's a garage with space for three cars. I park my brother's beat-up Fiesta in the drive and check myself in the mirror. I'm clean, but realizing that I'm likely underdressed in my high-waisted jean skirt and white tank top. A friendly black lab bounces up to the car as I open the door.

"Kobuk! Come here!" a woman's voice yells from the front door. I reach out to pet the dog, who wags its tail at me before obeying and turning towards the door.

The foyer beyond the massive door is larger than my bedroom. A giant grandfather clock betrays my late arrival by a minute past the scheduled appointment, but the white-haired woman doesn't seem to care. She offers me lemonade, that she pours from a crystal pitcher on the kitchen counter, and leads me to a small study filled with books. She offers me a seat on a leather chair. I sit and look around. On a bookshelf, I notice a picture of her with a young girl; they're wearing matching dresses with pink bows in their hair. The girl's hair is black as the mother's is white. I start to ask her about the picture, but she interrupts me.

"Leda, is it? That's an unusual name." Mrs. Woodruff leans over a glass of lemonade in her linen suit and pearls. I shift in my seat, smoothing my skirt. I feel extremely out of place.

"I guess. My mom found the name in a magazine and wrote it down. Then she dreamed about me, and the next thing she knew she was pregnant."

"Is that so?" Mrs. Woodruff's lips form a small, flat smile. I'm embarrassed, as if I've told a secret, even though I've heard Mom tell the story the same way a million times. Maybe it's her story to tell, not mine. "Have you ever thought about growing your hair out? I mean with such an unusual name . . ."

"No," I reply, feeling a scowl cross my face. She takes a sip of lemonade and switches gears.

"Of course. I think your short hair is quite flattering. Why don't you tell me about your experience with children?" she says.

I take a deep breath and regroup. I need this job. I need to figure out how to get her to like me. I stretch my legs out and look around the room a little more. Family pictures are nestled into the corners of shelves: black and white photographs, faded color snapshots, and professional shots framed in silver. In a wooden frame an elderly woman and a very handsome guy sit together on a deck, beaming at the photographer. They look like people I wish I knew.

"Well, I've done a lot of babysitting for my mom's friends." I have to stretch the truth a little. A lot really means three. "At first, I was a mother's helper, and then I started getting some regular customers. I brought a list of their names and numbers for references." I reach into my backpack, pull out the lined notebook paper, and hand it over. Mrs. Woodruff looks over the names. Oh god, I should have typed it and printed it on nice paper. But Mrs. Woodruff smiles warmly at the names and doesn't seem put off.

"Thank you. That will be helpful."

"And I'm an artist," I blurt out. "Would you like to see my portfolio?" I grab my phone and bring up the photos of my studio art.

"An artist? How wonderful. Yes, I'd love to see your work." She takes the phone from my hand and taps through the pictures. Her face lights up with interest.

"Delightful," she says, handing it back to me. "Now, tell me, what are your worst habits? And what would your mother say are your worst habits?"

What? "My worst habits?" I ask. "I'm not sure I know what you mean."

"You know, when you're at home, do you leave your dirty dishes in the sink? Forget to do laundry? Eat all the chips and leave an empty bag in the cupboard? Smoke behind the house where your mother won't see you? What are your worst traits? I want the truth now," she says smiling, "because if I'm going to have you living with us for the summer, I need to know what to expect."

"Oh. Well . . ." I stumble at the question. How honest should I be? I can't tell her that I lie to police officers and cover up hate crimes. I picture my room, not a complete catastrophe, but certainly not sparkling clean. There are a few dirty dishes by my bed. I hate to dust, but don't mind vacuuming. I've never smoked cigarettes, but I did smoke weed twice: once when I was bored, hanging out with Kira in her uncle's basement, and once when I wanted to make David mad. I'm pretty sure Mrs. Woodruff doesn't want to hear those stories.

"Come on now, Leda. Fess up." Mrs. Woodruff is grinning at me now, encouraging me to spill my guts.

"Well, I like to bring a late-night snack to my room, and I sometimes forget to take care of my dirty dishes. But eventually I do."

"Ha!" She gives a short laugh and smiles. "You call that a bad habit? You must be a responsible type."

"Maybe," I say. Except for the lies that keep pouring out of my mouth. "I suppose I am. Isn't that who you want taking care of your daughter?"

At that moment, a petite girl with long, curly hair, olive skin, and dark green eyes bounces into the room with a Barbie doll in one hand and box of doll clothes in the other.

"Mama, can you put a new outfit on her?" she asks, taking no notice of me. Mrs. Woodruff looks at me and smiles.

"I can help you," I say, reaching for her box. "Which sort of outfit do you want her to wear?"

Maddie turns to me with a bright grin on her face. "The pink dress, please." She pulls it out of the box and holds out the doll and her new outfit. "Who are you?" she asks, grabbing a lock of her hair and twirling it nervously around her fingers.

"I'm Leda," I answer. "I was just talking with your mom."

"Do you like Barbies?" she asks. I nod and smile as I pull the doll's dress over her silky, blond hair.

"I do," I say, "but I like art more. Do you like to paint pictures?" Maddie nods her head and then snatches the dressed doll out of my hands.

"Thank you!" she says, and sprints out of the room.

"Maddie, come back in here and say goodbye," Mrs. Woodruff commands, but the girl has darted away, and I can hear her footsteps disappearing up the stairs and into the depths of some far-off room.

"Well, that was my high-spirited daughter, Maddie. She seemed quite comfortable with you. I'll be honest, Leda, I haven't had a lot of calls for this position, and we're getting to the end of the school year. I could find a professional nanny through one of those agencies in Burlington, but I really think a local girl will do a better job, especially one who is creative. I can purchase some art supplies for you to use with Maddie, if you let me know what you need. I'll have to call your references and I'd like to meet your parents, but if all checks out"—she pauses and looks directly into my eyes—" then you are hired." We leave for the lake June fifteenth and will return to Mount Lincoln on August fifteenth. Will that work for your schedule?"

I'm stunned. I didn't expect her to give me the job on the spot. Now what? I sit for a moment before I realize I need to respond to her question. Dates, that's right. Eight weeks from the middle of June to the middle of August.

"Great, um, my mother and brother . . . I mean, I live with my mother and my brother. My father, he died when I was young," I reply, though I don't need to be telling her this.

"Oh, I'm so sorry, dear." But she doesn't give me the usual child-with-a-dead-parent-look most adults give. "Yes, I'd like to meet your mother and brother before we whisk you away." She looks at me expectantly, waiting for my assurance that this is all good. It dawns on me that I just accepted a job without asking how much she is going to pay me.

"Um, I was just wondering about payment."

Mrs. Woodruff narrows her long lashes thoughtfully. She looks as though she's considering my worth. My heart picks up its rhythm a bit. Isn't it normal to want to know how much or little I'll be paid?

"I mean . . . Is it an hourly rate, or a flat rate for the summer?" I stammer and my voice squeaks.

"$4,000 for the summer," she states, "with one weekend home at the end of July. I'll pay for your transportation costs home, and if you do an exceptional job, we can renegotiate your fee. Are those acceptable terms?"

If I try to find a job in town, which will probably be minimum wage, there's no way I could pull in that much. Granted, I would be home to hang out with my friends, but eight weeks isn't the whole summer. I'll still have two weeks with them. $4,000 is way more money than I've ever had.

"Yes." I smile back. "Yes, that would be great."

"You know, Leda, raising a child in your thirties is easier than in your late forties and early fifties. I don't have the same energy I had with my son." She points at the guy in the photo. "He's in college. Maddie deserves to have someone play with her, not just read books. I'm good for about forty minutes before she wears me down. Her father is an attorney and he works on cases all the time, even at camp, and my mother, we call her Gram, she's happy to help out, but she's eighty now, and I worry that she'll break a hip or something pretending to be an evil wizard. Having someone to be with Maddie during the day to help her stay busy will be a big plus for all of us. You'll love the lake. Do you swim?"

I think back to the reservoir. "Yes, I swim," I admit. "But I'm no lifeguard."

"Not necessary. Maddie is an excellent swimmer. But you'll want to do some swimming and boating, no?"

"Sounds great," I smile as I push the memory of the reservoir away. "I used to go canoeing with my dad."

"Really? Well, we have several kayaks and canoes, even a small sunfish if you sail. The camp is on the north side of the lake. You can't get there except by boat."

No access to roads. No way to come or go unless you have a boat. Safety from the outside world hounding me. And David won't just show up, he can't. This will give me time to think, time to figure out what to do. How to get out of this mess.

"Does that worry you?" Mrs. Woodruff asks. I look up at her, refocusing my attention on her pearls.

"No, it sounds just right, actually," I proclaim, and relax my face as much as possible.

Mrs. Woodruff looks thoughtfully in my direction. "Is there any reason I shouldn't hire you, Leda?" My face flushes, and I cast my eyes towards the framed pictures on the mantel. I could come clean now and tell her about the trouble I could be in. But what good would that do? I may not be involved at all. For all I know, it will blow over by the time I'm back.

"No," I say firmly, and meet her hazel eyes. "I am the best choice for this job and I promise, you won't regret hiring me." She nods and reaches out to shake my hand.

I rush back home, thrilled with myself. This is perfect. I can earn good money for the summer, get away from this crazy mess David has dragged me into, and somehow put my life back on track. I know this is the place for me. Distance will give me freedom. And I can paint. Mrs. Woodruff was impressed with my drawings. I only showed her some of my work, but Winnie, as she asked me to call her, was so gracious and supportive. She said she'd get some supplies so I can give Maddie art lessons. Imagine, me, an art teacher! I'm exploding with ideas and I begin mapping out lesson plans and themes for the summer: one week on collages using nature, leaf prints, and sticks, and another focused on landscapes and watercolors...

When I enter the house, I don't even notice my mother waiting at the chipped Formica kitchen table, coffee mug in hand.

"What's up?" I ask cheerfully, moving past her on my way to my room.

"Officer Templeton called and said they're pressing charges against David and MJ."

I halt my course and spin around to face her. Her lips are pressed tightly together, and I start to feel panic rise in my chest.

"What? Oh my god. Why are they doing that?" My mind is whirling, and I immediately start thinking about my conversation with the cop at school. What did I say? Did I say something that made them think David and MJ were guilty? I can tell from the look on Mom's face that David's arrest isn't her main concern.

"And?" I ask.

"And . . . I need to know what the risks are here. Is David going to offer anything to the cops about me?"

"Of course not. Why would you think so?" My attempt to defend David's honor is weak. The truth is, I'm not sure.

"People in trouble sometimes do whatever they can to get themselves cleared. I can't afford to lose the extra income if you want to go to college. And where would you and Keegan go if I ended up in jail?"

"Oh god! You're worried about me now? I have Keegan. He wouldn't let me starve. He actually cares what happens to me!" I clench my jaw against my yelling, but I know I've hurt her. The bird clock strikes eleven and a hermit thrush sings. I watch her smoke her cigarette. Her straight, graying hair hangs loosely around her face. She looks older than I remember. Maybe it's been a while since I really saw her. She's wearing a torn black sweater even though it's almost eighty degrees outside. A fan blows stale smoke around the room, but the doors and shades stay drawn.

"I don't know, Mom. I honestly don't think David is going to say anything. As long as I'm his alibi I don't think he'll snitch on you."

"Leda, they must have found some evidence that ties David to the crime." She stops and takes a deep breath.

"Officer Templeton said they'll be asking you to testify." The words flatten into the smoky air. I choke and cough, and then wave my hand as if I can make what she just said disappear.

"What if I don't want to?" I ask.

"Then they'll call you as a hostile witness. But it doesn't matter, you'll have to testify in David's defense, so either way you'll be on the stand."

I consider this. There's no way out, just like Keegan predicted.

I can't freak out in front of Mom. "When's the trial?" I ask, my stomach knotting up. My summer plans, my dream job, my escape.

"Sometime in August. No date's been set yet. They'll do an arraignment, but they don't expect it to go to trial for a few months. Honey, the officer did say it won't take forever because this case is so public. There's lots of pressure to get it in front of the judge before school starts up again. Even the university where David got that scholarship is pushing for a quick outcome."

My mouth goes dry. David will be on trial, and I am going to have to testify. Then it will be up to a jury to decide his fate, and maybe mine.

"I interviewed for a summer job today," I say, trying to sound casual, reaching into the cupboard for a box of cookies to snack on.

Mom looks at me with curiosity.

"What kind of a job?" she asks.

"I'm going to be a nanny. It's at a lake house."

"For who?"

"The Woodruffs, Winifred and Oliver. They're from Middlebury. They have this summer camp up north and

79

they need someone to take care of their seven-year-old for the summer. It pays really well."

"What do you know about being a nanny?"

I hear her tone. Everything shifts and I suddenly I feel small, incapable. When I was little, Mom warned me not to leave the house alone because I might get stung by a bee, or bitten by a snake. Despite my father's lessons in the wilderness, it still feels sometimes like the world is too much to handle.

"I've babysat before," I defend, but she's right, I don't really know much about seven-year-old girls.

"For a neighbor after the kid was already asleep. You ready to spend all of your waking hours with a child on your heels?"

"Joey didn't always stay asleep. I had to put him back in bed a few times." I'm filled with indignation. "Besides, I like kids, and Mrs. Woodruff wants me to give art lessons. It's going to be great." My determination falters a bit as I see the look on my mom's face. Heat rises to my cheeks.

She sighs. "If you think going off to some lake is going to get you out of this mess, you are sorely mistaken." She is staring at the blue wall above my head. Silence fills the room. "What will David say?" she says finally.

"About what? Me going away for the summer? I don't really care." I try to sound sincere.

"Well, you better care. You could get dragged right along with him, and me, too, for that matter."

It always comes back to her. "This isn't about you, Mom. David doesn't have any reason to rat on you."

"He does if he thinks you aren't going to back him up."

"So, what are you asking? You want me to stay? To protect you?"

"It's not just for me. It's our life. It's your art supplies, and your art school, and clothes, and food. My income keeps this family going." Her voice grows quieter, but it has a razor's edge.

"You can't lay that all on me," I whisper, tears brimming. My face feels hot. Her eyes meet mine and then she gets up and walks out of the kitchen and into her bedroom, jerking the door closed behind her.

Part Two

PERSUASION

✦

THE
NORTH WIND
AND
THE SUN

✦

THE NORTH WIND AND THE SUN were quarreling
with much heat and bluster. While they fought back
and forth over which of them was the stronger, a traveler passed along the road wrapped in a heavy cloak.

"Let us agree," said the Sun, "that the strongest one
can strip that traveler of their cloak."

"Very well," growled the North Wind, and at once
sent a cold, howling blast against the traveler. The wind
whipped the ends of the cloak about their body, and so
they shivered and wrapped it closer around them. The
harder the Wind blew, the tighter they held it to themselves. The North Wind tore angrily at the cloak, but all
his efforts were in vain.

Then the Sun began to shine. Her beams were gentle, and in the pleasant warmth after the bitter cold, the
traveler unfastened their cloak and let it hang loosely
from their shoulders. Then the Sun's rays grew warmer
and warmer. The traveler took off their cap and mopped
their brow. At last they became so heated that, to escape
the blazing heat, they pulled off their cloak and threw
themselves down in the welcome shade of a tree.

*Gentleness and kind persuasion win where
force and bluster fail.*

✦

8

Leda Keogh

THE TRAVELER

A S I SLIDE MY LEGS out from the warmth of the covers and search for my slippers, I see a black spider moving her way across my headboard. I hate spiders, but I'm learning to cohabit because there are just too many of them to kill them all. And, as Maddie informs me helpfully, they eat the biting bugs I also hate. I grab a plastic cup next to my bed and scoop the spider up, sprinting carefully to the door of the cabin and shaking her outside.

"If you stay out of my space, I'll leave you alone," I scold, feeling the urge to shake out all my limbs. I watch her quick legs carry her between the cracks of the porch and down below. Back to her family.

Family. My mom wouldn't look at me when I walked out the door last Thursday. I told her I was still David's alibi. That I wouldn't let him hurt her to keep himself safe. David told me he would drive me over to the Woodruff's, but when he didn't show up by nine thirty like we planned, I called the house and his mother answered.

"He went over to MJ's house," she explained. "He must have forgotten." I'm pretty sure he didn't forget. He's been avoiding stuff like that. So I just stood there in the living room feeling lost, while my mother sat in front of the TV watching *Grey's Anatomy*, acting as if I was just catching a ride to school and not leaving for the next two months.

"I'll take you," Keegan offered. Keegan to the rescue. He grabbed my bags and helped me out to the car. I turned to look at the front door, half hoping.

"She's just scared," Keegan said.

"And she thinks I'm not?"

He just shrugged. "You're doing the right thing. It'll be good for you to get away. Winnie seems really nice."

Keegan promised he would send me a text now and then, but so far, nothing. I don't expect my mom to send me care packages, but she could at least try. When I was little she used to play board games with me, and we would bake brownies together to share with my dad and Keegan. That seems like a lifetime ago. My dad's lifetime. She changed so much after he died. It's not like we were the perfect family back then, but at least we were there for each other.

I sweep my hand through my hair to shake off the feeling of rejection and slide back under the blankets for a few minutes. I've been here a week but I can't sleep in like I could at home. I think about Jonathan and Ricky all the time. I heard from Kira that Ricky went home from the hospital the week before I left. I should have called him.

But I do love living here. My room is amazing. It's like a damn museum. The cabins were built in the late 1800s, so every detail makes me feel like I've stepped back in time. The dressers have stenciled, winged tops and the small writing desk is made of old, dark wood and has a creaky wicker-caned chair. The lampshades look like paper, but when you get up close to them you can tell they're made of hide from some animal, tanned so thin they're translucent. Over the wide-planked floor sit worn rugs. They look handmade, and the biggest has a scene of children playing in the woods. The two smaller ones have animals on them: a bunny and a horse. This cabin was used by Mr. and Mrs. Woodruff when their oldest, Oliver, was small. Now it's Maddie's and mine. Maddie is thrilled we're sharing it.

The camp is made up of ten different cabins. There's a kitchen and dining cabin that has an old, black cast-iron stove, probably one of the first models. At first, I thought we had to make a fire every time we wanted to cook, but then, thank god, Maddie pointed out a regular stove in the corner. In the dining room, there's a huge oak table covered with a cotton tablecloth. Maddie loves being my tour guide. She knows a lot of the history for a seven-year-old. Apparently Gram, who arrived the day after we did, taught her well.

There is a flock of stuffed birds on the ceiling of the dining room: terns, gulls, grouse, pheasant, owls, and something else I can't remember. You name it, and it's been stuffed and hung on the Woodruff's ceiling. Maddie told me that some of them have been dead for a hundred years. Now that is plain gross. Who wants a century of dusty feathers hanging over your meal? What if one of them falls into the soup? I hunch slightly over my plate whenever we have to eat in there. Thankfully, we eat out on the deck a good deal of the time. It's wonderful out there. I love seeing the families of loons and ducks swimming by, circling ripples in the water until they dive for a meal. I could sit for hours watching them.

My favorite building is the rec cabin. Maddie isn't allowed to play in it unsupervised, and it is fabulous. A symphony of instruments is available to play, and if you'd rather listen to music, there's an old turntable and a collection of about five hundred record albums. Real vinyl, from Led Zeppelin to the Beatles to *The Sound of Music*. While we listen to songs, Maddie and I love to play pool. She has a better shot than I do, and the stick is almost twice her height.

The only downfall is, again, the dead animals lining the walls. There are some cool old snowshoes made from leather and catgut, but on either side are the heads of deer, moose, and bear, all killed in the woods around the lake. The moose is so large that it looks like it broke through the wall. Maddie has them all named, as if they're pets that will someday come to life and eat grass out of her hands.

"This is Pierre the Bear. He's my friend, and he always protects me. This is Oscar. He's cousins with Rudolph." She giggles. "And this is Pete. He's the moose and he doesn't talk much cuz they cut out his tongue. See?" And she proceeds to reach her hand inside the tongueless mouth. "Gram says they ate his tongue, but I think the cat got it."

"Why do you think that?" I ask.

"Because that's what people say: cat got your tongue. Not the people got your tongue and then they ate it."

I laugh at her logic, but nod. "I guess you must be right, then."

In the reading corner, there are Native American artifacts from the local Abenaki tribe. They're beautiful and look ancient. Maddie whispers around anything you can't touch. A beaded leather dream catcher hangs above the oversized chair near an open window that lets in the hum of the crickets. I wonder if I should bring it over to my cabin for the summer to see if it will take my bad dreams away. Maybe we could make them for our next art project. I lean in close to look at the mechanics of putting one together.

Next to the chair and lamp are three stuffed bookcases. Maddie brings over her favorite, a book of Aesop's fables. I laugh out loud at her choice. "Really? Your favorite book has the same name as the lake?"

"Yes." She insists we read some right then and there, and that is what we do.

9

✦

Jonathan Tanner-Eales
RESTLESS WIND

THE MEDIA ATTENTION has become a nightmare. I used to think that I would love the attention, cameras capturing my every move. But this—this sucks. Since the reporters are forbidden by the doctors to speak with Ricky, they hound my family. Every day we come home and find a dozen messages: *Do you wish to make a comment about the current status of the police investigation? Can you share Ricky's progress? Do you have a community of support reaching out to you? What do you think about the laws on hate crimes and harassment in Vermont? Are they strict enough? Are you pushing for harsher penalties for offenders? Some even have the balls to ask really personal questions: Did you always know you were gay? How did you come out to your parents?*

My mom says she knew I was gay before I knew the

difference between boys and girls. It didn't matter. I've always been able to make friends. Some of the boys kept their distance, or teased me for wearing button-down shirts to second grade, but girls adored me because I'd play dress up with them all day. Mom said I was never afraid to play the princess or the prince.

In middle school when my friends started hooking up, I told my mom and dad that I wasn't interested in anyone. At one point, I even admitted that the people I liked didn't like me back. My mom knew these "people" were boys, but she never said anything. Even though my parents were still married at the time, I came out to each of them separately. They didn't need any more reason for an argument. My mom and I were at my favorite coffee shop. I was thirteen, but getting more confident in myself. I had already stepped onto a stage. My birthday was coming up, and I wanted to go see an off-Broadway production of *After Midnight*.

"Is there anyone special you want to bring along?" Mom asked. "We can get an extra ticket." I remember just staring at her as if she could see Jacob's freckled face and piercing gray eyes running through my head. My face turned beet red until I realized that she hadn't said a girl, specifically. And when I thought about it, I realized she had never pushed me towards dating, or finding a girlfriend. She had just let me be.

"I'm gay," I said, without looking up from my caramel mocha. It just came out. Simple as that. And then the silence. When I finally looked up, she was smiling.

"Thanks for telling me," she said. "Do you want to bring anyone with you to the play?" I remember smiling such a goofy smile, relief and happiness bursting from my chest and bubbling up to my cheeks. It was as if I had just told her I was wearing purple socks. No big deal.

"How about Jacob?" I asked, and she nodded her approval.

Of course, once you tell one parent, you can usually assume that they will tell the other. Not so with my folks. They spent very little time together. In fact, it took three weeks after my birthday to be in our home alone with my dad. He had come to the play with us and was very nice to Jacob. Jacob wasn't out to his family at all, so we kept our crushes deep down.

That afternoon, Dad was in his home office, and as I walked past his open door, he asked me to bring him a glass of water. It was the first thing he had asked of me in a long time, and I remember being anxious to please him. "Sure. Do you want ice?" I asked.

"No, just tap water is fine," he answered, keeping his eyes glued to his screen. When I walked into his spaces, I always felt out of place, as if I had stepped into a stranger's house. I was never allowed in his office because I might mess something up. But by the time I returned with the water, Dad had opened the blinds on the window and closed his laptop. He took the water and invited me to sit down, gesturing to the chair nervously.

"Is everything okay, Dad?" I asked hesitantly, and frantically replayed my previous week in search of some wrongdoing I'd committed.

"Sure. I just . . ." He trailed off. "I just wondered if you wanted to tell me anything." Now I was certain I'd broken something, or Mom had told him how I'd eaten up all of the bread in the house. She was always complaining about how much I ate.

"Anything about what?" I asked.

"Well, um," Dad stumbled, folding and unfolding his hands in his lap. "I just thought, you know, that you and Jacob. Ah. That he might be your—"

"Oh! That!" I exclaimed. I realized Mom must have clued him in. I reached for my neck, feeling slightly dense. "Yes, well, sort of. I mean, I didn't know that you knew, so I didn't want to . . . ah, sorry." Every movement I made seemed to make my father sit back farther into his chair.

He rushed to get the words out. "No, that's okay. I didn't mean to bring it up out of the blue, I just thought you would want to know that I knew."

"Yeah, that's cool." I didn't know what else to say.

"Okay. Good." He nodded his head. "Good." He looked back up at me, clearly uncomfortable with this whole conversation.

"Great. Well, thanks, Dad."

"Sure. Thanks for the water," he said, holding up the glass to me like a toast. I stood up and headed toward the door, but then I twisted around, thinking I should clarify the whole Jacob situation.

"Dad?"

"Yes?"

"Ah, Jacob, he's not really out with anyone. I mean, can you not—?" I didn't even finish my sentence before Dad began to nod rigorously.

"Of course, of course. No problem. Who would I tell?" He chuckled nervously.

"Right, well, thanks," I said, and escaped as quickly as I could.

There's a white van from WPTZ parked across the road from our driveway, and we can see a small group of reporters with camera equipment and microphones. They want to know everything. For a small community, this is a big story, and they just won't leave us alone.

We stop answering the phone. Memorial Day weekend I thought the media would take a break, but they just kept calling.

"I want to have the landline shut off, Mom," I say. "We don't really need it. We have phones, we have Internet—what's the point?" Mom agrees for the most part, but she hesitates.

"Let's get out of here, okay?" she suggests.

"Where to?" I'm very ready to get away.

"How about the camp?" she offers.

"Fairyland?" I almost laugh.

"No, it's a real place! Where my cousin lives for the summer. She has plenty of room, and she invites us every spring and I never take her up on it. But I think this is the perfect year to get out of here. To clear our heads."

"What about Ricky?" I ask.

"You said he's doing better, right?" She ends with a question even though I know she's spoken to Rita. She knows he's improved a lot over the last week. I still go to the hospital, to check in, but I don't go into the room. It just makes me feel better to be close by.

"He's starting to talk more, but he hasn't talked about that night yet."

"Well, that will come when he's ready. But you don't need to be with him until the day he's released. I think you need a break, and his parents will certainly understand. You can check up on him from the camp."

"I guess," I concede. She pulls me into a quick hug and I tense up a bit, but I don't pull away. We've never been a huggy family, but I really appreciate her attempts to connect with me.

"Okay then, it's settled. I'll let my cousin know! It will be fun, just wait and see."

10

✦

Leda Keogh

THE SUN

A<small>T FIRST,</small> I carry my phone all around the compound hoping to hear from David.

"Hey what's up?" I text, but get no response. I send pictures of my cabin, the lake, and Maddie. Finally, after a few days of silence, he responds.

"You'd really rather spend your summer with that kid than me?"

I take a few deep breaths before responding. "It pays really well and I'm going to need the money for college."

He doesn't write back. So I stop texting him. It's a risk, but I need a break so I can think straight. I ask Keegan to check in with David, and to tell him we're having a problem with our Internet.

David and MJ are being charged with assault with a deadly weapon, and since it's considered a hate crime, the penalty could be pretty steep. He has to work at the garage all the time to pay for his attorney fees. He is an amazing mechanic, can fix anything. Of course, his dad totally expected him to take over the family business, but David really wants to be a mechanical engineer. Most of the kids don't even talk about college, they just want to work on the farm, or have babies. I can't picture that life without feeling cornered, and I can't picture David behind bars. I'm pretty sure he'll get off. It's their word against ours.

MJ's mom told the cops she checked on her son at 9 P.M. and he'd fallen asleep early. But MJ, being MJ, bragged to his teammates that he's ridding the school of queers as his final gift to the student body. It was a stupid thing to say even to his buddies, because someone told the cops. I guess MJ cares more about his image than his future.

It's easy to spiral into worry from the latest stats on hate crimes and bullying . . . I go searching for it, which I do. I read story after story. Kids who were harassed in their schools. Kids who committed suicide. Kids who were beaten and died. Thank god Ricky didn't die. I also read about the people who commit these crimes. They are often religious, like David, or Alt-Right assholes, more like MJ.

Thankfully, Maddie wants to be with me every moment of the day, which helps. It's easier to be around kids sometimes. I catch myself trying to avoid having conversations with Winnie and Gram. Gram, especially, seems like a really interesting person, but I don't know what to say to her. I've never had grandparents. Gram takes a walk at seven every morning. I've watched her from my cabin as I get Maddie ready for the day. Gram is three inches taller than me, with a full head of silvery red hair that shoots out all around her face. Sometimes it's wrapped in a scarf, and other times she winds it into a braid on top of her head. She has a broad nose, a pointy chin, and gray eyes. Her leathery skin is smooth and buttery. She always has a shawl on, and she wears pants, or as Gram calls them, trousers, and a blouse, otherwise known as a shirt. Her eyes are sharp, and I get the feeling that nothing really gets by her. She seems to know everything about everyone.

Gram uses a walking stick with a carved hummingbird on top. I don't know how much she actually needs it, but she seems to like poking at the bushes and clusters of puffballs. After her walk, she goes to the kitchen and fixes herself a bowl of cream of wheat with a dollop of yogurt, a spoonful of prunes, and a cup of coffee, black. Then she watches the news for an hour and moves to the deck on sunny days, or the rec cabin on cloudy days, to read until lunchtime, when we all eat together. Breakfast is on our own, and I eat with Maddie.

One morning Maddie sleeps in, and I'm finally getting the hang of rising early, so I find myself awake and hungry. As soon as I get to the kitchen I can smell burned toast. I stop in my tracks.

"Good morning," Gram says. The smell of the coffee fills me with comfort.

"Good morning. Sorry, I didn't know anyone was up yet." I hesitate to move forward.

"Well, I don't own the kitchen. You're welcome to come in and fix yourself breakfast anytime."

"Thank you. I guess I'm still sorting out what the rules are."

She smiles. "Yes, it can be tricky to try to find your way in a labyrinth."

"A labyrinth?" I look at her with confusion. Is she talking in parables?

"A labyrinth is a maze. Or don't they teach that in school anymore?"

"I know what a labyrinth is."

"You do. Oh good. Well, pour yourself a cup of coffee and let's talk about them for a while, shall we?"

I hate coffee. "I don't drink coffee," I say, and give her a polite shrug.

"You mean you haven't learned how to drink coffee yet."

"No, I mean, I've tried it and I don't like it," I clarify.

"And how did you try it?" she asks.

"I don't understand."

"What did you put in your coffee when you tried it?"

"Milk and sugar."

"And why did you add milk and sugar?"

"Because that's how my mother drinks it."

"And you are your mother's twin?" she asks, giving me a curious look.

"No, but that's how my brother drinks his too," I say, feeling this justifies my action. What does she have against milk and sugar?

"Ah, of course." Is she mocking me? It's just coffee.

"Well, how would you suggest I drink it?"

"Oh, it's not for me to say. But why not start with just black. See if you like the taste of the coffee itself." With that, Gram takes out two mugs, pours the dark liquid into each, and hands one to me. I take it and sip.

The warm bitterness hits my tongue. It smells strong, like I'm drinking it through my pores. I hate to admit it, but it's much better this way.

I look over at her. "Thanks."

"Winnie tells me you're an artist," Gram says, as we sit across the counter from each other.

"I love drawing."

"And you are going to study illustration?"

"If I get into college."

"Well, getting in should be no trouble. You just have to lie and tell them what a great kid you are," she says, eyes glinting. My jaw drops open like an idiot. Does she know? And then I see her smile.

"Oh! Thanks. Very helpful." I laugh nervously and look away. When we hear the creak of the screen door, we both look up to see a tousled head. Maddie is rubbing her eyes with a look of suspicion; we've been having fun without her.

"Why didn't you wake me?" she whines, and I hold my arms out to her. She scrambles up onto my lap. The wet dew of the early morning grass clings to her legs.

"Never wake a sleeping child," Gram says sagely, like she's quoting Lincoln. Maddie pouts back at her. Gram gives her a kiss and heads out the door.

"Leda?" Maddie asks.

"Yeah?" I look at her. She has the darkest brown eyes I've ever seen. And her nose is a sharp little point, just like Gram's.

"What are we going to do today?" she asks.

I think a second. "Well, I thought we might storm the castle later this morning."

"Storm the castle?" Her eyes grow huge.

"Haven't you ever stormed a castle before?"

"I don't know what that is," she replies, confusion and wonder growing on her face.

"Well, then you are in for a fun day. It's one of my favorite things to do, and I've been waiting for a special day—I think this is it!"

"Why's today special?"

"I heard that the king and queen are away, and every peasant knows that the best time to storm the castle is when the king and queen aren't at home."

"Okay! How do we do it?" Her eyes are shining.

"Oh, that will take some careful planning. We'll need the right costume first. Do you have camouflage clothing?"

"I don't think so." Maddie taps her finger on her chin thoughtfully. I don't think she really knows what camouflage is.

"Okay then, we'll just have to make our own. Let's find the darkest, greenest, brownest clothes you can, and then we can work on blending into the woods. And I think I know exactly how we can make a bow and some arrows."

"Bows and arrows? What do we need those for?" Maddie's eyes become large ripe olives.

"To show our strength when we storm the castle, and in case we need to defend ourselves or take hostages," I say, looking as tough as possible.

"Whoa," she breathes. This is going to be fun. I quietly thank my dad. I was so young when he taught me survival skills, but I paid attention, and so will Maddie.

Winnie and Oliver Senior left early this morning to go through the Fables, as the lakes are nicknamed, and drive the sixty miles to Plattsburgh to pick up their son, Ollie, from the airport. He's flying in for the Fourth of July. His arrival will spark a flurry of preparations for the Independence Day celebration on the lake. As I'm told, it is the event of the summer. Ollie just finished his freshman year at Washington University, the "Harvard of the Midwest," or so Winnie keeps saying. Pictures of Ollie are all around the kitchen and the dining room. I try to be objective, but the reality is that he is gorgeous. Dark, curly, black hair, much like Maddie's, and eyes that look like a smooth, dark chocolate river. He has strong cheekbones and a hint of freckles. He always looks relaxed and confident in the pictures. Even his senior photo, a shot of him standing against a tree in a pair of jeans, is stunning.

Maddie and I spend the morning writing a ransom note for Kobuk, the black lab. We hope to exchange the dog for lunch. We build bows out of aspen saplings and arrows from the forsythia's naked limbs. Then I scoop some dark mud from the lake into my palm and begin covering Maddie's face. Her little body wriggles with excitement.

"No one ever lets me put actual dirt on my face!" she grins. "They always tell me don't come to the table until your hands are clean." She mimics her mother's facial expression and I grin, too, despite myself.

"Do you think Gram will recognize me?" she asks with such an earnest expression that I have to swallow a giggle.

"Well, I don't know. She might mistake you for a mountain girl." I smile at her and the two of us sling our bows onto our backs. I grab a handful of arrows and tuck them neatly into the old oatmeal container strapped around my shoulder. We move from building to building, listening to the sounds of the birds and the crickets. We dash behind trees and make secret signals to each other. When we reach the kitchen cabin, I place a finger over my lips and withdraw the ransom note. It's about ten thirty now, and Gram is lying on the sofa in the dining room, her long white hair unpinned. Fortunately for us renegades, Gram is already snoring Kobuk lies on the rug in front of her.

"I'm going to get a treat for Kobuk. You place the ransom note on Gram's lap without waking her. Can you do that?" I whisper, and Maddie nods her affirmative. Her small hand grasps the paper as she moves towards her grandmother. I can tell Maddie is determined to be as quiet as the wind in the grass, but just as she steps on the floor in front of the sofa, the boards squeak and Gram's eyes fly open. The old woman grabs Maddie's wrist.

"Eek!" screams Maddie.

"Ah-ha!" Gram yells. She scans the ransom note. "Thought you would break into my castle to steal my dog, eh? I've dealt with the likes of you."

Maddie is wild-eyed with excitement. "Leda, Leda, she's caught me! Help!" I run to the door, but instead of Maddie, I see Ricky sprawled on the hallway floor of the school. I blink and the memory fades, but a feeling of helplessness rises up.

I whistle to Kobuk and hold out a treat. Kobuk comes running, and I snatch his collar, trying to remember our plan. "Let her go!" I yell, but my eyes are stinging with tears and my heart is racing. Gram peers at me over Maddie's head, concerned but still playing along.

"Okay, all right," she says, "let's do a trade. You can have the little girl and the dog but first you'll have to—eat my cooking!" Maddie and Gram scream in horror and start laughing. The noise shakes me back into myself.

"How bad can it be?" I ask, but this only sends the two rolling on the floor.

"We'd all starve," Gram chuckles. "I don't cook." They continue to laugh and I take a deep breath, smile, and turn toward the kitchen to find us something for lunch.

Winnie and Oliver arrive by motorboat in the late afternoon with the Adonis. At least that's my first impression. He's a god. I catch his dark eyes as he looks up to see Maddie waving. I hold my breath. He doesn't give me a second glance, instead shifting his gaze to his little sister. He grins a display of perfect white teeth.

The second they dock, Maddie hurries over to her big brother and hurls herself into his arms. She is beside herself with excitement. He crouches down to her level and talks with her. They're being silly. I envy their relationship and feel an ache for my own brother.

"Ollie!" Maddie squeals. "I missed you!"

"I've missed you, too, squirt." He looks over her head and casts a suspicious look at me. "Who are you?" How kind.

"Ollie, don't be rude," scolds Winnie. "This is Leda, Maddie's nanny. She's been with us for two weeks now, and we love her. She's one of the family. I'm sure I told you about her."

"I'm sure you didn't," he replies. "Why does Maddie

need a nanny? I never had a nanny, and I managed to keep myself busy just fine."

"Oh, Ollie, really. Leda, this is my headstrong son, Oliver, who doesn't think I do anything right when it comes to raising children and one day will have a family of his own just so he can prove me wrong and raise his children the right way." With that, Ollie bends over and kisses his mother's cheek.

"So, Winnie brought you to Aesop Lake for the summer? I hope she's paying you well. She's loaded," he nods towards his mother.

"What?" I ask, surprised.

"Ollie!" Winnie grabs a small pillow off a deck chair and knocks him over the head.

"I'm sorry, but it's true. For someone to give up their whole summer to hang with a seven year old, you should be paying her more than minimum wage."

We all head up to the kitchen cabin. I can't help but notice Ollie's muscled arms and legs tensing nicely under his shirt and shorts as he climbs the stone steps. When we make it inside, Ollie stretches out on the sofa. Maddie pounces on his stomach like a dark-haired feline. I feel a blush creeping over my cheeks when he catches me staring at him.

Quick, say something. "Do you play sports?" I ask.

"Yeah, soccer and track. You?"

"I run, too, sometimes. But I've never been much of a team sports kind of person. I prefer art."

"How come?" he asks.

"I dunno. I guess I like to work at my own pace, and that's hard to do that on a team."

"Good point." He tickles Maddie under her arm, and she wiggles and squeals. I think of Keegan. We don't horse around anymore; it's hardly appropriate at our age, but I remember us wrestling when I was Maddie's size.

"Maybe we can take a run in the morning," Ollie offers.

"That sounds nice, but I'm usually busy with Maddie in the morning. She's wakes up super early. I get a break in the afternoon, though," I say, looking over at Winnie.

"Ah yes, Maddie practices her reading with me in the afternoon," Winnie offers. "Ollie can show you the trails then."

"Great," he says. "Three thirty?"

"That'd be great," I say, trying not to seem too excited. Or nervous. Ollie looks like he could run a million miles an hour.

✦

11

Jonathan Tanner-Eales

THE WIND

A N OLD-STYLE wooden motorboat careens across the lake toward Mom and me as the sun sets and a wave of mosquitoes drifts by. Six docks line up like floating tables, lamp posts at their ends to guide the boats to safety. Some have motorboats anchored to them absorbing the waves. A small duck family swims under one of the docks, and the mother dives to retrieve a morsel. The fluffy ducklings attempting to replicate her move without success.

"Isn't it beautiful?" Mom exclaims. "Just like I remember. I haven't been here for thirty years, but nothing has changed."

This isn't necessarily a good thing, I think. I like progress, though I suppose I can see the advantages of having your childhood memories still intact. I often wish for that myself. When the boat pulls up in front of us, a young man waves. He has dark, curly hair and looks like he stepped out of *GQ*. I hardly know this second cousin. He went to boarding school and is now in college in Missouri.

"Ollie! You've grown up so much!" Mom moves closer to the boat, pulling her suitcase alongside her while Ollie tosses a rope over the post.

"Yup, funny how that happens," he smiles and turns towards me. "Jonathan and Marcia, my long-lost cousins from Massachusetts! Welcome to the Fables." His tone is teasing. I like him at once.

"The Fables?" I ask.

"Yeah, we call these three lakes the Fables because of Aesop's stories. If you look at an aerial view of the lakes, you can see that they're shaped like a turtle, a hare, and a crow," he explains.

Ollie maneuvers the boat deftly across the water, rising on a wake, then veering through the corners through one passage after another. Finally we arrive at Aunt Winnie's camp compound. Mom has described the camp many times over the years, but her stories never overwhelmed my senses like the huge pungent pines swaying over the buildings, like sentries. Ollie pulls the boat up to the trout-shaped post and ties the boat to a brass ring. How fancy.

A woman walks lightly down the stone steps to the boathouse, her long, gray hair pulled into two braids. Her wrinkled skin is the color of lightly toasted bread.

"Look at the two of you! I can't believe you're finally here. My god, little Jonathan—is that you?" Winnie exclaims.

I blush, but welcome the warm arms the woman wraps around me. She looks relaxed and happy, like she's been on holiday for months. The magic here has clearly been working for her.

"Oh, Winnie, it's just like I remembered! I can't wait to show Jonathan around. Where is Maddie? I haven't seen her since she was born. How old is she now, five?"

"Oh dear, it has been a while. No, she's seven! She's having an art lesson with her nanny right now."

"Her nanny?" Mom asks, and Winnie gives us a warm smile

"Yes, we hired a girl to come stay with us for the summer. She's a darling, you'll love her. She's an artist and keeps Maddie busy with projects."

"Sounds like the perfect setup. So, what do you do with yourself all day?" Marcia asks.

"Oh, I find plenty to do: gardening, cooking, sleeping, reading. You'll see, the opportunities to relax are endless. Come on, let's get you to your cabins and you can settle in and then we'll have dinner." Ollie and I gather the luggage as my mother and her cousin link arms and make their way up the stone steps ahead of us. I linger for a moment, looking out at the water.

I turn to look at Ollie. "Do you spend every summer here?

"As much as I can. As a kid, we always arrived at camp the day after school let out and didn't go back until school started. But as I got older, I had sports practices that started up in August, and now that I'm in college, I barely make it here for a few weeks."

"That too bad," I say.

"Yeah, I miss the quiet. It's nice to get away. My mom said you grew up in Boston?"

"Yeah, up until last year, when my parents split up. Then Mom and I moved to Vermont."

"Do you miss the city?" Ollie asks.

"Sometimes. Vermont can be boring as hell," I say. "I miss going to shows and galleries and things." I hesitate, thinking these might not be the things that Ollie would miss. "And real sports teams, you know what I mean?"

Ollie nods and holds out a bag to me. "Well, at least we have the lake," Ollie says, and we head up the steps. I follow him, breathing in the earthy odors of pine and clover, lake water, and sunscreen.

The building at the top of the steps is built of logs. The window frames are painted green, and a tilted screen door hangs on the front of the cabin. It squeaks loudly as Ollie grabs the handle and pulls it open. Inside, the cabin is clean and cozy. An old tapestry hangs on the wall, and I study the scene: hunters firing and reloading as ducks rise to escape above the tree line.

"You okay, man?" Ollie asks, looking concerned.

Oops, I've been staring too long. "Yeah, I'm fine. Just taking it all in," I say.

12

✦

Leda Keogh

THE CLOAK

"LEDA, look at my painting!" Maddie stands back from the canvas and holds her brush out like a young Matisse. Her cheek is smeared with red where she wiped away a gnat, and the painting smock is spotted with a rainbow of colors, like a speckled egg in the tropics. She's always proud of her work, and I love to see her take it so seriously. I wondered if I could keep a seven-year-old entertained all summer, but art has become our way to connect.

I circle around my own canvas and look at Maddie's. We're working in watercolors, spending a good part of the week getting the feel of how colors mix with each other, and how to layer in the pale blues with the darker purples.

"Nice, Maddie! I love the way your trees are standing guard around the water's edge and protecting that boat."

"That's not a boat!" she exclaims.

"It's not a boat? What is it then?" I ask.

"It's a beaver."

"That's the biggest beaver I have ever seen. Wow!" I exclaim.

"Can we take it to dinner and show it to Aunt Marcia?" she asks.

"Of course." Company rarely comes, so its a big event for all of us. Winnie's cousin and her son arrived earlier today, and Maddie came tearing into the cabin wanting to paint them a picture. "Let's get our paints and brushes cleaned up, and then ourselves. We can pick some flowers to bring to your auntie, okay?"

Maddie wiggles from top to bottom. I love her. Everything about this family feels comfortable. They treat me like one of their own. Even Oliver Sr, who is absent most of the time, but pleasant enough when I do see him. Ollie and I run sometimes in the afternoons, but we don't talk much, just run together and then part ways. He's nice enough, though, and takes me boating when Winnie asks him. He's given me a few lessons so I can take Maddie out on the water. He's cute, so he must have a girlfriend, but he never mentions anyone.

Maddie leads the way down the stone path to the kitchen cabin. The windows of the dining room are lit up, and even though it's hours until sunset, there's a fire burning in the woodstove. Gram probably requested it; she doesn't like to feel the cool breeze off the lake without a warm fire.

As we step into the kitchen, Winnie comes through the swinging door with a plate of potatoes in her hand.

"Hello, you two. We're just getting ready to serve dinner."

"Maddie told me your guests are here," I say.

"Yes, and I insist you eat dinner with us, Leda. I think you may know my nephew. He might go to the same school that you do: Mount Lincoln High?"

That's random. "Really? What's his name?"

"Jonathan."

I stand perfectly still. I only know one Jonathan from school. My feet cement to the floor, and I sway. I can feel the blood draining from my face and pooling in my chest cavity. I reach out and grab the doorframe, focusing on it as I try to pull myself together.

I can't eat dinner with Jonathan. "I'm not really feeling well, Winnie," I say, covering my mouth and turning towards the door.

"Oh, sweetie, are you okay? Let me get you a drink of water. You probably just had too much sun today. Sit down in the rocking chair and take a break. I can get dinner on the table." Winnie ushers me to a chair and fills a glass with water. My insides are churning. What could I possibly say to Jonathan? He knows I'm David's alibi.

"Maybe I should lie down," I suggest. Winnie moves closer and places a cool hand on my forehead.

"You don't feel like you have a fever. Drink some water. I really don't want you to miss the first night of visiting, it's always the best, don't you think? That's when everyone gets to know each other. You'll feel left out."

"It's okay, I don't mind. I'll catch up tomorrow." I attempt to stand but Winnie gently pushes me back into the chair.

"Are you sure? I think you'll be just fine once we get a little food into you." She shuffles around the kitchen, grabbing serving spoons and platters of food. I inhale the scent of guilt and exhale shame. I give up and bolster myself to stand and go into the dining room. The light over the table is dimmed, and the wine glasses are set and filled. The cherry credenza is stocked with food: a roasted chicken, potatoes, beans, rolls, and cranberry sauce. Jonathan is filling his plate and turns to see me enter the room. Our eyes meet. A flash of emotion crosses his face, but he doesn't say anything. He swiftly turns back to the buffet and continues piling food on his plate.

"Marcia, I'd like to introduce you to Leda, Maddie's nanny."

Marcia shows no hint of recognition. She smiles warmly at me. "Very nice to meet you," she says. "I've heard you're wonderful with Maddie."

"Thank you. Nice to meet you as well," I say.

Marcia turns to her son. "Jonathan, aren't you going to say hello?"

"Hey," he nods in my direction, keeping his back to us. The back of his neck is bright red, but I can't tell if it's a sunburn.

"Hi," I reply. Winnie gives no notice to the strain in the air, but Ollie immediately looks over to me. He raises his eyebrows. Dammit. I shake my head and move to the buffet table with my plate. I try to make myself small and unnoticeable. Marcia picks up the conversation again, chatting with Gram about Jonathan's plans for the future. He wants to be a film director.

I feel an urge to break the tension. "I thought you

were really great in *The Music Man*, Jonathan," I offer. He whips around and glares at me. I take a step back, almost bumping into Ollie.

"Leda wants to be an artist too," Gram adds. "Visual arts. Isn't that right, Leda?"

I take a seat at the table, next to Maddie and across from Marcia. "Yes. I'm hoping to study art in LA." I push my food around my plate. The sooner it looks like I've eaten enough, the sooner I can be excused from the torture.

I watch Jonathan for his response. He picks up a chicken leg and brings it up towards his mouth, but then pauses and asks, "Isn't that where your boyfriend wants to play baseball?" His tone is measured. Now Ollie turns to stare at Jonathan.

"I don't know what David's plans are at the moment," I say, looking Jonathan in the eye. "He and I haven't been in touch much since I came to camp."

"Well, that's a convenient way to avoid the situation. Take a job on a remote lake and never answer your text messages."

"I'm not avoiding anything," I retort.

Marcia's face suddenly shifts. She's started to put the pieces together. She looks from me to Winnie, and then to Jonathan. I meet her eyes for a split second and then look down again at my food.

"I'm still not feeling well," I whisper to Winnie. "May I please be excused?"

"Of course, dear. Go take a rest," she says, reaching out to pat me on the back. She looks from me to Jonathan, but is too polite to force an explanation. I get up to leave the room and feel the heat of a dozen eyes following me. Maddie scooches her chair back and tries to dart toward me, but Ollie grabs her from behind and pulls her to his lap.

"Come here, peanut, you need to eat." I cast a grateful look at him and rush out of the room.

Outside, the fresh air feels cold against my flushed cheeks. I can't believe this is happening. This was supposed to be a refuge.

13

✦

Jonathan Tanner-Eales

THE CHALLENGE

LEDA RUNS out of the room and closes the door clumsily behind her. I look around the table.

"What? I just asked a question."

"Jonathan, I think you had better go talk to her," Mom whispers to me. Everyone else is staring.

"I'll go talk to her, but I can't promise she'll feel better." I excuse myself and go in search of Leda, hoping she is nowhere to be found. Unfortunately, I can hear her crying the moment I step out into the night air. The sound of her sniffles and sobs carry through the trees on the wind. I find her sitting on the steps to one of the bigger cabins.

"What do you want me to say?" I ask. I look down at her and shove my hands into my pants pockets. Her hands are wrapped around her face and she tries to wipe away her tears and snot.

"You want me to tell you I understand? That it must have been really hard for you to hear that your boyfriend beat the shit out of your science lab partner and you didn't know what to do? Are you going to tell me he beats you too, and that's why you had to lie for him? Otherwise he might hurt you? Or is it that you hate me as much as he does and you really just wanted it as much as he did? Maybe you were disappointed that I made it out okay, that I managed to swim far enough out." I'm furious. How dare she act like a victim.

"Stop it! Please, just stop it. I don't know what you want me to do. We weren't there. I wasn't there, I promise."

"Oh, please, Leda. I know it was David and MJ."

"What? How?" she asks. She must be worried I have proof.

"I know their voices, Leda. How many times have they yelled shit at me at school? Do you think they changed their voices that night at the reservoir? Maybe I can't prove it, but I know it was them. And you gave him an alibi! You told the police he was fucking you on Tully Hill. You're such a liar; you know he was kicking the shit out of Ricky."

"I don't know anything! Stop saying that!" She's crying harder now.

Whatever. I turn away and head back into the dining room. There's no way I'm missing dinner for her. Someone slams a door in the distance, and I shake my head. She's such a coward. When I come back to the table, Mom looks at me nervously. I roll my eyes and head for the chocolate cake sitting on the buffet. The table is cleared of chicken and potatoes and everyone is digging into their desserts. Ollie is playing music from the speakers, which takes the edge off, and the atmosphere lightens. Winnie moves to my side, gently touching my arm.

"Should I go talk with Leda?" she asks. I shrug my shoulders, unsure how much to share.

She nods. "Okay, I'll give her a little space first."

I load a fork with chocolate cake, filling my mouth so I don't have to reply.

14

✦

Leda Keogh

WARMTH OF THE SUN

THE CRICKETS grow louder and the water laps at the shore's edge. I sit on the front porch of my cabin. It's the kind of night that deserves a selfless gesture or a lover in the moonlight, but I just feel abandoned. I let everyone down. I'm certain Winnie will be asking me to pack by morning. Jonathan probably went back to the dining room and told them the whole story.

"Hey." I hear a voice and look up through the towering pines. Ollie stands there looking a bit disheveled.

"Here to help me pack my bags?"

"Are you going somewhere?" he asks, taking a seat on the steps next to me.

"Your mom's definitely going to fire me."

"This is a big place. I'm sure you can keep out of Jonathan's way, if that's what you need to do," he says.

He turns towards me and looks straight into my eyes. He's very close.

"What?" A feeling of guilt and discomfort spread across my neck and into my cheeks.

"You look like you need to make a confession," he says.

"Are you a priest?" I ask, and silence sits between us. Ollie waits. "Maybe I do. But I can't."

"Don't you get it?" he says, his knee bumping mine. "That we like you, that no one wants to see you upset? Well, except maybe Jonathan. But the rest of us, we like you."

"You wouldn't say that if you knew me." I want to talk to Ollie; I want to tell him everything that happened that night. Something tells me he wouldn't judge me too harshly. But I can't. If he goes back to Jonathan and tells him, then everything will fall apart. My mother might go to jail, and we could lose the house. And Keegan can barely support himself, let alone me, so I might end up in foster care, like my friend Carrie. It would all be so much worse than just living with the lie.

"What is all of this about, Leda? I didn't even know you have a boyfriend," he says.

"I don't know if I do," I hesitate, not wanting to give details, but wanting to make Ollie understand I'm not really a bad person. "I mean, Jonathan doesn't understand the whole story, and I can't really explain it."

"What do you mean?" he asks with such genuine concern that I tell him the simple version of what happened to Jonathan and Ricky.

"Jonathan is convinced that David is the one who did it, but I was with David, so it's not possible," I lie and look away from Ollie, because now my lie is spreading into this relationship. I can't keep expecting everything to hold up, and yet I can't stop myself.

"Why does he think that?" Ollie asks.

"Because David isn't very nice to Jonathan or Ricky. He's really religious, and he thinks that being gay is a choice, that it's a bad choice."

"And what do you believe?"

"I don't know. It's not my business. I don't know, my parents never took me to church or read the Bible to me. I'm not saying David's family is right, but they have beliefs. And they take it more personally, I guess. David and his parents, they look at being gay as being really sinful."

"That's pretty religious," Ollie says.

"I guess, but it's also kind of nice know what you should believe. I mean, it's all laid out for you in the Bible, like a how-to book."

"Have you read the Bible?" he asks, looking at me with a puzzled expression on his face. "Because I have, and it is not a how-to book." He snorts and looks in my direction.

I feel a little bit warmer inside. "Well, you know what I mean. I just can't fault him for his values."

"Unless those values hurt other people, " Ollie suggests.

"I guess," I whisper, but my thoughts are far away. I think about David's family, the prayers before meals, the crosses hung around the house, the Sunday services. They have such strong values. But his parents say cruel things to him sometimes. It's confusing, but when I ask David about it, he just gets defensive and says they're doing their best to make sure he turns out to be a strong person. Spare the rod, spoil the child, and all that.

Strangely, I feel still, like the top of the lake. "I don't want to go back to Mount Lincoln."

"Does that mean you're going to stay?" He looks at me, hopeful. His leg is touching mine and I can feel how warm it is. It feels wonderful. What about David? Why did I say David was my boyfriend? We didn't exactly break up, I just stopped texting him. I've been keeping my distance, just like Keegan told me to do. *And now there's this amazing boy.*

I make up my mind. "If your mom wants me to stay, I will."

"She does, and so do I," he says, touching my elbow with a warm hand, "and so does Maddie."

Just then Maddie comes racing up to my cabin steps, her face smeared with chocolate frosting. She's carrying a piece of cake on a paper plate along with a glass of frothy milk.

"I brought this for you!" she proclaims. "I think it'll make you feel better. Mommy says you have a tummy ache. I told her chocolate cake will make it feel better."

I smile at her. How could I even consider leaving?

15

✦

Jonathan Tanner-Eales
GENTLE BREEZE

IN THE COOl of the morning, the fog is just lifting off the lake. I stretch my legs over a chaise lounge on the deck and sip Earl Grey tea. It looks as though the Fourth of July weekend is going to be perfect weather, except for the storm brewing between Leda and me. I don't want to cause problems, and certainly don't want the cousins to get the impression that I'm a complete ass. I made the decision last night before falling asleep that I would enjoy the week and do my best to avoid any more arguments. She's their employee, and I'm not expected to spend time with her, just tolerate her politely at meals. That's fine. I can do that. Thankfully, there are other people to hang out with, and I do want to get to know Gram, Winnie, Ollie's dad, if he ever stops working, and Maddie—and Ollie seems especially nice.

"Hey," Ollie calls, arriving with his own cup of hot liquid, sporting a pair of swimming trunks and a gray sweatshirt. His curly hair sticks out in all directions and I wonder if it's intentional.

"Hey. Morning," I reply.

"I was thinking about taking one of the kayaks out. Care to join me?" Ollie asks. I've never been in a kayak before, but I'm pretty certain I'd eventually get the hang of it.

"Yeah, sounds great. When?"

"After eggs and bacon." Ollie gives me a smile as Winnie comes through the screen door with two mounds of scrambled eggs layered with crisp bacon and buttery toast.

"Thank you!" I grin at Winnie and she smiles back.

"Eat up. It's a great day to get out on the lake before it gets hot. Ollie can take you over to Doleba Island to swim." I haven't gone swimming since that night in May and my stomach clenches a little. Boating is one thing, but swimming . . . My flesh prickles with the thought of treading water. I shake my head to empty the memory from my brain and take a bite of toast to calm my gut.

"Doleba Island?" I ask.

"Yup, it's one of the little islands out in the middle. It's shaped like a turtle—the name's Abenaki," Ollie offers. "You'll see. Takes about twenty-five minutes to paddle over to it." We sit together, wolfing down protein and carbs in silence. I don't want to admit I'm terrified to swim again, so I swallow my eggs and feign excitement for the day ahead.

By the time I change into swimming trunks, Ollie has already put the kayaks in the water and found two paddles and life jackets to use. He motions me toward the green kayak with the yellow pinstripes down the side, while he grabs the blue kayak with an eagle feather painted on top.

"Can you swim?" Ollie asks.

"Course. But I've never been in one of these."

"You'll catch on soon enough. I'll hold onto yours while you get in, just keep your center of gravity low and move slowly. Kayaks are tippy, and not very forgiving if you flail around."

I do as Ollie suggests, and before I know it I'm tucked into the belly of the kayak with a life jacket snapped tightly around my chest and a paddle in my hands. Ollie, in the meantime, slides gracefully into his vessel and begins lobbing instructions to me. It sounds like a foreign language: ports and starboards, bows and tips. I nod and smile, pretending I understand.

We begin paddling and I find I like the rhythm, the pull of the water with the paddle, feeling my weight move under my own strength. The tip of the paddle swirls in the water and my muscles burn happily. I do my best to stay close to Ollie. He's wearing only his swimming trunks; his life jacket is tucked behind his back like a pillow. He looks rather all-American. I don't hate it.

We stay within a hundred feet of the shoreline, and I'm able to see into the depths of the wooded banks and forest surrounding the lake. We pass several other camps along the way. Most are newer than Winnie's, and some look as though they're still under construction.

I'm now keeping good pace with Ollie, who slows a bit so we can carry on a conversation.

"Who lives there?" I ask, pointing to a camp with modern architecture and a grand deck that juts over the water.

"The Yens," Ollie replies. "They bought the land from the McGovern's about five years ago and have been adding a building each year. They seem nice enough, though we miss the cookouts the McGovern's held every year for the Fourth of July." A girl in a pink bikini lies out on the deck. She looks out to see the kayaks, shading her eyes from the sun. Ollie gives a wave with his paddle and yells a greeting. The girl stands up, frees her long black hair from its ponytail, and leans over the railing to wave hello back.

"You know her?" I ask.

"That's Kim. She's a sophomore at Dartmouth. We hung out a bit last summer, but her parents are super protective. I dunno, it's not like we were going to get married. We're still friends, but I keep my distance," Ollie says and looks a bit mournful as he waves farewell. We continue paddling toward the island.

The wind whips across the open water from the south end of the lake, and we use every ounce of muscle to push our boats forward. By the time we reach Doleba Island, my shoulders are burning. I'm hot and ready for a break.

Ollie pulls out a thick rubber bag that's holding trail mix and water bottles and a few apples dry. I lie on a flat rock at the edge of the island and tip my head back.

"How do we get home?" I laugh. "I think I may have to stay here forever."

He chuckles. "Well, you could try. There are lots of rabbits to eat on the island, but they're fast little bastards."

Ollie tosses the trail mix onto my lap. "Here, have some water and snacks."

We eat and drink in silence. The sun is warm on my chest as the day begins to heat up. It doesn't feel too hot, but the potential is there.

"I'm going to swim. You coming?" Ollie asks.

I feel my pulse quicken and my heart pound. "I don't know," I hesitate. I feel Ollie's gaze on me, but I can't look him in the eye. "I haven't been swimming since—," I break off and look out at the water. I'm pretty sure Leda told Ollie the story. Ollie stays silent for a moment.

"No worries," he finally says, and dives into the water, disappearing for what seems like a very long time to me. When at last he surfaces, he's far from the shore. He waves and shakes the water from his eyes and hair.

I consider my predicament. Here I am, on a beautiful lake, and there are no assholes around. I am safe here. But I'm still scared. Really scared, actually. I decide not to swim, and instead focus my energy on pulling up the grass around me stalk by stalk.

After a while, Ollie swims back to the shore and pulls a towel out of another rubber bag. He dries off and appears content and unconcerned that I chose to stay ashore. "Leda is coming," Ollie reports. This takes me by surprise. Why would Leda be coming out this way? When I look out over the water, sure enough I can see her and Maddie in a wooden canoe paddling toward us. Maddie is waving madly. She's a sweet kid, but kids are annoying. They're cute enough from a distance, but really, they seem like a pain. I can't imagine wanting to have my own. But here they are, a seven-year-old and her babysitter. I squint and try to study Leda's face as they come into focus. She looks miserable and apologetic. Maddie looks ecstatic. It's clear that this was not Leda's idea.

Ollie waves back at his little sister with a broad grin on his face. He's not surprised by the turn of events. For all I know, Ollie told Maddie to paddle out and find us. I watch Ollie as he smiles at Leda, taking her in like a welcomed warm breeze. I wonder if there is more to it than just friendship.

"She's such a brat," Ollie says of his sister, but with a huge grin on his face. I nod silently in agreement. "I bet she dragged Leda out here," he adds, cocking his head.

"I'm sure," I agree without dispute.

16

✦

Leda Keogh

PERSPIRATION

I KNOW JONATHAN wants nothing to do with me. When I woke up this morning, I was so happy that Jonathan and Ollie had taken off in the kayaks. But Maddie was miserable.

"Why did they leave me?" she cried. "Why didn't they ask me? I can paddle with Ollie!" Winnie did her best to console her daughter, but Maddie was determined to make all of us miserable. When she stormed off, I was sure I'd find her in the rec room listening to records. She's not allowed to be in there by herself. Instead, Maddie made her way down to the boathouse. I have no idea how she managed to get the canoe from its rack into the water, but there she was, roping the boat to the horn cleat and gathering the paddles and a life jacket. She was going after them.

"I'm going paddling," she says, arms folded firmly in front of her, a determined expression on her face.

I stand and look at her from the bottom of the stairs. I sigh inwardly. "I wasn't going to try to stop you, Maddie. But let's pack a little food for the trip."

"You're going to come too?" she asks, her eyes lighting up. The scowl washes from her face.

"Well, of course. I can't let you go on an adventure without me. Plus, I think your mother would want us to stick together."

"I can paddle the canoe by myself," she declares, daring me to challenge her.

"I bet so," I say. There's no point in arguing.

"And I know how to swim," she reassures me.

"Yeah, I know. I've been swimming with you, remember?"

"Oh, yeah." Maddie hesitates and looks at the canoe and then back to me. "Let's get some snacks."

After we pack a bag with peanut butter and jelly sandwiches, apples, and bottles of fresh water, Winnie lays out strict rules to Maddie about keeping safe. Then the two of us set off. Marcia lingers by the boat launch looking anxious. I know she wanted this to be a day for Jonathan to get away.

"Don't worry," I say in her direction. I can't help myself. "I won't do anything. I'm well aware of how Jonathan feels about me, and I have no interest in making things worse." I know I'm being a brat, but I am being honest.

Marcia holds my gaze for a moment, her silver-striped bangs falling over her narrow eyes. She nods and turns away. I grab my life jacket and gently slip into the back of the canoe.

By the time we reach open water, Maddie has given up paddling. Her arms are tired. She sits in the front eating an apple and sipping water. My arms ache from fighting against the strong winds, and I consider telling Maddie that I can't get us to the island on my own.

"What do you think they're doing?" Maddie asks.

"I don't know," I huff. "Probably exploring the island."

"Maybe they're swimming," Maddie suggests. I think about this, wondering if the last time Jonathan went swimming was that night in May.

"I doubt it. But we'll see," I say.

When we get close to the island, I spot the boys. Jonathan is sitting on a boulder in the sun, and Ollie is waist deep in the water. I search Jonathan's face for a reaction. I try to project my regret to them both. I really was trying to avoid them.

Maddie stands up in the boat to wave to the boys, and her sudden movement tips the canoe to the left. When she tries to recover her balance, the boat rocks back, and all of a sudden she's in the air. I watch her scrabble and reach forward to grab her shirt, but she falls into the water, banging her head on her paddle as she goes under. The boat rocks back, and I tumble out of the other side. I feel my foot catch on the seat of the canoe and it flips behind me. I go under, and then my life jacket yanks me back to the surface and I can hear Maddie crying. I swim towards her. Thank god she's wearing her life jacket. I hear a splash from the distance and in a second Ollie and Jonathan are there. I put my arm around Maddie and Jonathan paddles near me, looking scared. We all swim towards shore. Maddie is in her brother's arms. We reach the rocks and Jonathan races back out to retrieve the canoe and oars.

Maddie has a small bump on her head that's swelling.

"You need to be careful!" Ollie yells at me.

I freeze. "I'm sorry. I didn't know she was going to stand up in the boat."

"She could have been seriously hurt." Ollie glares at me. Like I could have prevented a seven-year-old from being impulsive.

Maddie sits on one of the large rocks wrapped in Jonathan's towel, gently touching the egg forming on her head. "What does it look like?" She's recovered quickly and now seems proud she has something to report to her mother and Gram.

"It looks like a turtle laid an egg on your forehead," Ollie teases, relieved. Maddie giggles, and I'm filled with happiness. She'll be okay. My vest is dripping onto my legs and getting cold, so I take it off and drape it on a bush to dry out in the sun.

Jonathan has said almost nothing since he came out of the water. His silence is a vacuum. I'm so scared to address him directly, so instead I try to pick up the conversation with Ollie and Maddie. "Maybe if you wait a few weeks, it'll split open and a baby turtle will crawl out," I suggest. On second thought, that sounds kind of ominous.

"Could that really happen?" Maddie asks, full of wonder. She's the best. She presses her small hand to the bump, feeling for the baby turtle inside.

"No, silly," Ollie replies.

"I wish I were a turtle," Maddie says.

"Don't be so sure," says Ollie. "Remember the tortoise who didn't want to walk slowly anymore, so he decided to fly like an eagle?"

"Mm, yes. What did the tortoise do?" Maddie asks. I'm pretty sure she knows this fable by heart, but Ollie scoops her into his lap. Jonathan gets up and walks to the edge of the water, pitching stones across the surface. I watch him move farther away from us.

"An eagle carried the tortoise high into the sky and then let go, and the tortoise smashed to the ground into tiny pieces," Ollie finishes, and Maddie nods approvingly. Weird kid. Then she huffs a little and jumps up to stick her toes in the water. Ollie looks over to me and tilts his head in Jonathan's direction, as if I should go over there and talk to him. I shake my head in response, scowling.

I'm suddenly exhausted. I turn to Maddie. "Let's get ready to head back to camp, okay?" It's going to take forever for me to paddle back, and I feel bad following Jonathan who is clearly trying to get away from me.

"No!" she wails. "We just got here!" I look to Ollie for backup, but he just shrugs. Jonathan has come back within hearing distance, and I see his shoulders slump.

17

✦

Jonathan Tanner-Eales

WRAPPING THE CLOAK TIGHTER

"LET'S TAKE A LITTLE HIKE, and I'll show you the top of the turtle's back," Ollie says to the three of us. I reluctantly fall in line since it appears the girls aren't going to get back into the canoe and head home. I consider climbing back into my kayak and heading to camp on my own, but I'm feeling stubborn. This is my vacation, after all.

"Hold my hand, Maddie," Leda says, reaching out, "this trail is slippery." I notice the wetness of the leaves on the forest floor and the moss growing on the rocks and trees. The light dims under the dense foliage as we make our way up the trail. Ollie grabs his little sister up and plunks her on his shoulders. She laughs with delight and turns to look behind her at Leda.

"I'm taller than you!" she declares the obvious, and I try to force a smile to my lips.

Leda doesn't have to. She clearly enjoys the silly games. "And you have two heads. Are you a serpent from the lake?"

"No, I'm a Sasquatch!" Maddie says, and Leda feigns a fearful expression.

"If you're a Sasquatch, then you'd stomp all over us." And on cue, Ollie begins stomping his way down the path, raising his arms and moaning like a Neanderthal on the loose. Maddie joins in and starts making deep throaty sounds that remind me of a frog more than a monster, but the effect of the two together is ominous.

I watch this whole exchange and feel nostalgic. A story is being played out that I can't become a part of. And it's not that Leda and Ollie are leaving me out. I could join in. But I feel so removed from everything. I'm nervous all the time. And I feel like I can't pretend anymore. Everyone's always pretending. The monster isn't some giant creature on an island, it's actual kids who go to my school.

"Get them! Get them!" Maddie roars and Ollie turns to chase Leda and me. When he storms towards me, I freeze, and feel anger and fear exploding inside.

"I don't want to play your stupid game!" I shout, and take off at a run up the path, pushing branches out of the way and trying my best to jump over tree roots and stones. I put some distance between us and slow down. Now that the rage has subsided, I feel stupid. I just ran away from a boy with his sister on his shoulders. They're probably laughing their heads off at me. My breath comes hard, and tears fill my eyes.

When I reach the top of the hill, I look out over the vastness of the lake. The small whitecaps on the surface look like cappuccino foam. What would Ricky say right now if he was here? When he finally found his voice, he asked me to go away. From behind, I hear a branch snap and I turn, half expecting an animal. Instead, I see Leda approaching cautiously. Ollie and Maddie are nowhere in sight.

"What do you want?" I ask, hoping she'll back off and disappear.

"I need to talk to you," she says, looking resolute.

"I already told you, Leda. I don't want to hear your bullshit."

Her face is strained. "I know. I can't do it. Everything has consequences, and sometimes the consequences are bigger than we think they are."

"You aren't making any sense, Leda. Go back to your fantasy world where you make up the rules."

"That's not fair, Jonathan. If I could do it differently, I would." She's pleading now.

"Whatever, Leda. You only care about yourself. You're so fucking selfish. Or maybe you think David is your ticket out of here. But he's not. It's obvious."

"Jonathan, there are things you don't understand. Things someone like you or Ollie will never understand, that you won't ever have to face." Her mouth twists.

"Tell me then!" I shout at her. "I'm all ears! Tell me about it! I don't think you've had to deal with shit."

"That's not true!"

"Yeah? Try being gay in this town. You wouldn't last a second." My breath is coming hard, and I glare at her until she looks away. She turns. Clearly, she has nothing to say.

At last I hear crunching footsteps. Ollie is holding Maddie's hand as they step from the shadows with some trepidation.

"Hey," I say, trying to sound conciliatory.

"Are you okay, Jonathan?" Ollie asks with genuine concern.

"Yeah, I'm okay. I guess I just freaked out a little bit there." I hold a hand out to Maddie. She reaches up and squeezes it.

"I get scared of monsters too, Jonathan," she offers. "It's okay."

"Thanks," I say.

"Hey," Ollie says, looking at the three of us, "let's get back to camp. There's lots to do before for the party tomorrow."

Maddie jumps with delight, like this is the first she's heard of the party, and goes bounding back down the trail. Leda follows silently.

Part Three

UNITY

✦

THE
FATHER
AND
HIS CHILDREN

Λ FATHER HAD TEN CHILDREN who always fought. When his yelling and punishments failed to settle their arguments, he decided to give them a practical illustration of the evils of disunion.

He told them to bring him a bundle of ten sticks. When they did, he placed the bundle into the hands of his youngest child, and ordered her to break it in half. She tried with all her strength, but couldn't. He then placed the bundle into the hands of his second-youngest child. He tried as well, and failed. And so on and so forth. None of his children, even the oldest and strongest, could break the sticks.

The father opened the bundle, separated the sticks, and placed one in the hands of each of his children. The sticks broke easily. "My children," he said, "if you are of one mind, you will be safe from your enemies. But if you are divided, you will break as easily as these sticks."

In unity is strength

18

✦

Leda Keogh

SNAPPING STICKS

BY THE TIME we arrive back at the camp, it's late afternoon. The weight of Jonathan's words and Maddie's refusal to lift a paddle slowed us down. I see Winnie on the kitchen deck, and as soon as she spots us in the distance, she begins waving and hooting. She hurries down to the boathouse to help.

"I fell out of the boat, Mommy," Maddie tells her, and Winnie immediately looks to me.

"She stood up too fast, and we both fell. Thankfully, Ollie and Jonathan were right there and helped pull us to shore," I quickly explain.

"I'm glad everyone's okay. So you made it all the way to Doleba Island? Wow, that's a distance. You must be exhausted," Winnie exclaims, wrapping Maddie in a big hug.

"Not really, Mommy, it was fun. But I did get a turtle egg on my head," she says, and lifts her hair to show her swollen forehead. It looks a bit better than it did, but will definitely be a marble color by tomorrow.

"Oh my goodness! Look at that. You had better put some frozen peas on it. And go ask Gram to give you some Advil, okay?" Winnie pulls the life vest off Maddie and sends her up to the kitchen cabin for repairs.

"Are you okay?" Winnie turns to look at me.

"Yes, I'm fine," I reply.

"Is everything okay with Jonathan?" she asks.

"Well, not so much. But I don't blame him."

Winnie gives me a once-over.

"He can't like me while this whole mess is still happening. I understand that," I say.

"Well, I hoped you two could become friends, because really, from everything Marcia has told me about Jonathan, I think you have a lot in common."

I stare at Winnie and then shake my head. He's the last person in the world I want to be friends with.

"Now, about thirty people are arriving tomorrow to eat and watch fireworks. So we have plenty to do to get ready."

"Oh, I didn't know we were going to have fireworks!"

"Mr. Yen hired a guy to set them off from over there," she says, pointing out a clump of trees jutting out of the water, "so we invited everyone here. I think we have the best view of the island from our deck. We'll need some help with food prep and setting up the chairs, if that's okay with you. I'll get the boys to give us a hand as well."

"Great," I respond, just as Jonathan and Ollie pull up into the boathouse. They gave Maddie and me a head start back to camp.

"You're just in time," Winnie exclaims, and I head off toward the kitchen without waiting to hear their response. I guess it's good that a bunch of people are coming over. It sounds as though there will be other kids around as well, so Maddie will have some buddies to hang out with. If I'm lucky, I can disappear to my cabin and watch the fireworks from a distance. I don't really feel up to being in a huge crowd.

The next morning, we're all assigned jobs. Even Maddie and Gram have corn to husk and hamburger to shape into patties. The boys get busy filling the coolers with ice and beer from the cellar. Red and white wines are dusted off and displayed on the bar.

Before the first guests arrive, I have cleaned and chopped a variety of fruits and vegetables, made dip, arranged bowls, cracked ice into buckets, and draped the tables with clean tablecloths. This picnic has become more of a feast. A spiral ham is laid out in one corner, and a huge punch bowl is filled with fizzy juice and an ice ring with little plastic stars frozen inside. Red, white, and blue serving dishes have been pulled from deep within cabinets. Gram brings out a bag of firecrackers and sparklers that I arrange in a bouquet for guests to take when the moment is right and the night sky sets in. I'm starting to get excited.

Mr. Yen and his wife and daughter arrive by motorboat. I count seven other moorings and wonder if there will be enough places for everyone. Mr. and Mrs. Yen are beautiful, both with high cheekbones and translucent skin. Their daughter, Kim, has long, silky black hair that cascades over her shoulders. I wonder if this is the girl Ollie means when he talks about Kim. A sudden pang of jealousy rises as I watch them hug. It's clear they're close.

Guests continue to arrive, and Winnie introduces me to everyone as "Leda Keogh, who is staying with us for the summer," instead of as the nanny. It's nice, but I feel suddenly and defensively proud of being a nanny. There are three kids from New York—Damien, Rachel, and Oscar—who are all under the age of eleven. They're quick to find Maddie and scamper off to play until the fireworks begin. A middle-aged couple follows, dragging along the woman's sister, Agnes, who looks like she'd rather have stayed home and read a good book. I see her moments later petting Kobuk and chatting happily with Mr. Yen, so maybe she's accepted her fate. I try to figure out what each couple does for work and decide that most of them come from money. They act like they've been comfortably wealthy for generations. A couple named May and Langdon are the last to arrive with their son, Andrew. Andrew looks a couple years older than Ollie. He looks unhappy to be here but is handsome in a cool, let-me-run-my-own-life kind of way. I see May whisper to her son and nod in Ollie's direction. Ollie is talking intently with Kim and touches her arm softly. She's smiling at him. I watch as Andrew shakes his head at his mother, then moves away from her towards the bar and pulls a beer out of the cooler. Jonathan has managed to disappear either into the crowd or back to his cabin. I make my way over to the bar area with my cup of punch.

"Hey," I say to Andrew, and smile up at him. Ollie's clearly busy, and Andrew seems like the most interesting person to talk to.

"Hi," he replies, and his eyes catch on my chest on their way up to mine. I blush and look away. I don't have much to offer in that department.

"Do you know Ollie?" I ask, trying to make conversation. It's not my strong suit, and I feel out of practice.

"For a while, yeah. I don't remember you. Are you new to the lake?" he asks.

"I am. I'm Maddie's nanny for the summer."

"Nice. She's a lucky kid. Want a beer?" He's talking to me but looking past me over my shoulder. This boy is not good at eye contact. I blush more.

"No thanks, I've got a drink." I hold up my cup, gesturing to the obvious. He reaches up and rubs his stubbled chin, as if deciding if punch constitutes a real drink.

"Okay, I get it, you're a law-abiding young adult," he grins. It's a nice grin.

"It's not that. I just, well, I'm responsible for Maddie, and I don't want to . . ." I trail off. I look over at Ollie, who is still talking with Kim. He clearly doesn't care what I'm up to.

"I better help out with the food," I say.

"No, don't go," he says, stepping forward.

I glance around the room. "Um, I need to go," I state, and walk past him, slicing through the Yens and making my way to the kitchen. Andrew turns his head to follow me. His hair flops over his eyes and he reaches up and pushes it to the side, giving me a wink. He smells like cigarettes and a little bit like sweat. My stomach feels kind of wobbly.

I find Gram pouring a bit of vodka into her punch cup. "Now you know the secret to a long and happy life," she smiles, and I laugh nervously.

"Do you think I'm needed any longer, Gram? I'd really like to watch the show from my cottage. The scene's a little much in there."

"Is there a scene? And I'm missing it. Damn." Gram beams happily. "You can leave anytime you like, my dear. You've done plenty today and earned a night off."

"Thanks," I call, already halfway through the back door and disappearing into the night. I weave my way along the quiet earth and sit on my small deck and listen to the hub of the party carry across the water. Everyone seems to be having a good time. The troupe of kids is playing flashlight tag, and occasionally I hear one of them scream as they're caught. When at last the fireworks start, I feel sleepy and wrap myself in a blanket. It's so nice to curl up on the wicker sofa and soak in the richness of the sky. The display is beautiful, and so bright against the dark, dark black. With no city lights to mute the colors, the sparkling blues, reds, greens, and yellows explode and I feel as if I could reach out and grab them.

The first time David and I were alone together was a year ago tonight. Mom wouldn't let me date anyone until I was sixteen, so when David first asked me out, I had to say no. But I turned sixteen at the end of the school year, and when I ran into him during Old Home Day on the Fourth, I was so happy. He invited me to sit with him for the fireworks. and we spread a blanket in the crowds of people and watched the bursts of color above us. It was so romantic. We had our first kiss that night, and I never wanted it to end. David smelled like a garage and tasted like cotton, but he rubbed my back but didn't try to go any further. I felt safe with him. On the way home we talked about everything. I told him about my dad dying when I was young, and he told me about his family and his mother's battle with breast cancer, how they were close, and how it was important to him that his family meet me. It was all so sweet. I finally feel peaceful. My eyes feel heavy and I drift off to sleep in the warm breeze.

I wake up to hot air on my face. It smells like beer. I freeze and then open my eyes and see Andrew leaning over me. He kisses me and it's sloppy. His hand pushes my shirt up towards my breast.

"What are you doing?" I cry and grab his hand, the one that's under my shirt. He straightens up and looks at me. Then he kisses me again. His mouth is warm and wet. I taste beer and cigarettes, and I feel like I'm going to pass out. I push him away again.

"Get off of me!" I shout at him, hoping to jolt him out of his drunken stupor.

I try to slide backwards out from under him, but he puts his hand on my hip. I'm scared and confused, and now I can barely move. I shove him again and unwrap my legs from the blanket.

"Come on, baby, you're so beautiful. I saw the way you looked at me." He pins my thigh with his knee and now I really can't move. It hurts, but I almost can't feel it at all. He reaches down, and I see his jeans are already unzipped and loose at the waist. He pulls his penis out through his boxers. I try not to look, but I do. He sees me do it.

I feel his hands groping at my breasts and then down to my crotch. I finally scream, and it sounds garbled and far away. I can't catch my breath. The weight of his body is pressed against me—and all at once he's on the ground. Jonathan is on top of him, pounding Andy's face with his fists. The noise is awful. Andrew isn't fighting back at all. His head looks like a tetherball. I take a deep breath. Suddenly, I can move. Anger is moving my limbs like a puppet. I push myself toward the twist of bodies on the floor and yank Jonathan backwards with all my might. He isn't ready and falls onto his back on the deck, his arms still in front of him. He looks a like a turtle. I kick Andrew's stomach with all my might. I feel pain flare through my big toe.

"Ouch! Oh shit," I yell, and Jonathan sits up and looks up at me, as if he's surprised to see me still in the room. I grab my toe, just as Ollie runs up the stairs.

19

✦

Jonathan Tanner-Eales
STRENGTH

I'm losing interest in the party. I watched the fireworks, and now everyone is just drinking and making small talk. I'm tired of small talk. I see two people gesturing in the shadows, and one of them points towards Leda's cabin. One of them walks towards it. I'm pretty sure it's Ollie. I wonder if Leda is cheating on her asshole boyfriend. I don't give a shit.

I consider telling Ollie all about his new sweetheart and feel some satisfaction. Then I hear a scream. It doesn't sound real. I don't know if anyone else heard it, but how could they not? No one comes running. Then I realize it has to be me. Jesus, the last thing I want to do is get involved.

I walk towards the cabin, and stay quiet to assess what's going on. And then I hear some guy. I think it's Andrew. My stomach turns, and my body freezes. I feel the cold water lapping my body again. What's happening? Is it something bad? My legs don't move. Then I hear furniture grating across the deck, and I hear Leda scream again.

I open the door and fly across the floor. My hands and arms feel super-powered. I can't let someone else get hurt. Andrew has Leda pinned to the couch. I grab him and pull him off Leda. I see her face. She looks confused and scared. I toss him to the floor, follow him down, and punch him with every ounce of anger I've kept inside. "Get off of her!" I hear myself shriek. I want to see his blood spill on the floor. I want this guy, Andrew, to feel fear. I want to feel relief.

Suddenly hands grab me from behind and pull me backwards before I can brace myself. A foot comes out of nowhere and lands in Andrew's stomach. He moans and it breaks my concentration. I sit up to see Leda grabbing at her toe. Her face is tear streaked and she looks furious.

Ollie runs into the room and sees Andrew, who isn't moving. "Holy shit! Are you okay? What happened?" I hear him like I'm underwater. He's muffled. All of time and sound travels in slow motion. I try to focus my eyes and take in my surroundings, but it's all blurry and completely senseless. I stand up.

Ollie pulls me into a chair, and the world stops spinning. My hands are ripped up. I'm not certain if the blood is mine or Andrew's. They hurt, so I suppose some of it must be mine. The adrenaline has dropped out of my body, and I feel weak and deflated. I look around and see other people gathered around Andrew and Leda. When did they get here? Ollie is next to Leda, who is sitting on the couch with a blanket wrapped around her. Winnie strokes her hair and rubs her back. She looks fragile. And still pissed. She's not paying attention to me, but I look away in case she glances up and catches me watching her. Andrew's gone. An older couple, they must be Andrew's parents, stand close together.

"We thought he was better. I'm so sorry. We thought he was better." His mother continues to speak rapidly but I tune her out. I hear the words "safe" and "public."

My mom steps onto the porch, taking in the scene. Her gaze lands on me and my bloody, swollen knuckles, my tear-stained face.

"Jonathan, what happened?" she cries, and I turn away, not wanting to see her worried expression.

Ollie answers. "That guy, Andrew, who was here for the party, he assaulted Leda." Mom's face drains of all color, and Ollie reaches out to hold her shoulder. "She's okay, Jonathan heard her yelling and pulled him off. But then he kind of let loose on the guy."

"You mean he hit him?" Mom asks.

Ollie nods, looking worried. He's not looking at me.

"Jonathan, honey? Are you okay?" Mom asks, kneeling in front of me. She puts her hand on my knee, but I push it away. She looks to Ollie, who nods towards Winnie.

"Winnie, what the hell happened here?" Mom demands. Winnie moves away from Leda and pulls Mom to the stairs and out onto the grass. Conversation on the porch quiets, and I can hear the whole thing.

"Marcia, I'm so sorry that any of this happened. I had no idea about Andrew. I think his parents thought it was better to have him here where they could keep an eye on him."

"What are you talking about?"

"This isn't the first time Andrew's done something like this. His parents just told me he's been charged with assault before. They didn't think he'd do it again. Andrew must have seen Leda leave, and he must have followed her. Oh god. I should have asked Ollie to walk her back to the cabin."

"Stop," Mom says, "just—where are his parents going? What happens now?"

"I've called the police. Andrew is going with his parents to the other side of the lake right now. Witnesses here can sign affidavits as to what happened. Please, Marcia." There is silence for a moment, and then Winnie continues, "I know Jonathan got hurt. I know you want to be there for him."

Ollie pats my shoulder. "I'll see you in the morning, okay? Maybe we can go for a hike."

"Yeah, okay," I reply. A familiar tightness in my chest. My hands are still bloody. Mom and Winnie are back up on the porch, and when I see my mother looking at them, I shove both my hands into the pockets of my hoodie.

"Will Leda be okay?" Mom asks Winnie.

"Yes, I think so. I'm going to sit with her awhile." Winnie leans over and places a kiss on my cheek.

"Thank you, Jonathan. I'm so glad you were there."

I nod, but look away. My mom leads me back to my cabin. We walk slowly, the silence only broken by our feet on twigs and pine needles. When we reach the door, she hesitates to follow me in. I go straight to the bathroom and run hot water in the sink, pulling my hands free from my pockets and placing them under the stream. The blood pools and swirls down the drain, and I remember my mom helping me wash my hands after finger painting. There are a few cuts, but most of the blood seems to belong to Andrew.

I scrub the crusted blood off and my mom hands me some soap. I wince a little, but after a couple of Band Aids my hands look almost normal. Back in my bedroom Mom turns her back so I can slide my pants and shirt off and crawl under the sheets. We still have not spoken, other than a few cursory words about towels and changing. Once I'm under the covers, she sits on the edge of my bed and smooths my hair away from my eyes.

"Good night, Jonathan. I love you." She kisses my forehead and shuts off the light.

"I love you, too, Mom." She turns to the door and leaves.

20

✦

Leda Keogh

SINCERITY

THE SUN'S RAYS slip into my cottage before I'm ready to give up the night. I'm feeling worn down, and my body aches. I can't even hear Maddie in the room next door. And then I remember the smell of alcohol and cigarettes, and the feel of sloppy lips. I bury myself deeper under the blankets. This place was supposed to be safe, a place where I could forget everything and all the shitty things people do to each other.

It's later in the day than I'm used to rising. Someone must have set Maddie up somewhere else for the night. I didn't think about her last night, not even to say good night. I hope she wasn't too upset. We didn't sing any songs or read any books together. I turn my head and see Winnie sleeping on the chaise lounge across the room, a patchwork quilt hanging loosely over her legs and a pillow propped under her neck. Gratitude spreads through my limbs like honey on toast.

I sit up as quietly as I can and gently place a foot onto the cold floorboards. My muscles ache. It took a long time to fall asleep, even with the sedative Gram gave me. When I finally lay down, Winnie sat on the edge of the bed and rubbed my back. She told me that everything would be okay, that I'm safe now.

I make my way to the bathroom. My eyes are bloodshot and a small lump has formed on the left side of my head where it hit the back of the couch. Now Maddie and I will be twins. That's something, I guess. My lips feel a little swollen, too, but I pretty much look the same. Nothing has changed. I let the pee stream out with relief and feel sadness take its place. Tears leak from the corners of my eyes.

I take a deep breath and make my way back into the room. I can do this. Winnie is up and folding her quilt. She turns to me as I enter.

"Good morning, Leda. How are you?" she asks.

"I don't know. Still dazed, I guess."

"Of course. It was a pretty rough night for you." Winnie sits on the edge of the bed and pats the blanket. I obey.

"I know that what you experienced last night was awful. I'm so sorry. If you don't mind my sharing, something like that happened to me when I was about your age."

"It did?" I ask, shocked.

"Yes. It wasn't a stranger—it was my aunt's boyfriend. He did things like making sure to touch the sides of my breasts every time he hugged me. I had to learn how to never to be alone with him. Then he had an accident and he died. I can't say that I was sorry. But I do remember being terribly frightened and feeling like I needed to check around corners for years, long after he was gone."

I sit in silence for a little while, contemplating her story. Winnie wraps an arm around my shoulder. "That must have been awful," I say.

"It was, but eventually I was able to move on. It took time. There's no time limit on these things. We all recover at our own pace and in our own way. There's no shame in that. You didn't do anything wrong, Leda. I should have never let them bring Andrew to the party last night."

I take this in. "I love having you here, and Maddie just adores you. But if you want to go home, I under-stand, and we will make the arrangements today. I'll still pay you for the summer, so you needn't worry about getting another job. If you want to go home and be with your mother and brother, that's fine. But I hope you'll stay. We want you to stay."

A million responses bubble up inside. Winnie is searching my face for an answer.

"Is it okay if I think about it today and then decide?" I look at Winnie. Her eyes are shining with tears

"Of course, dear, you can take as long as you like. Why don't we tell Maddie you're a bit under the weather today? You can stay here and rest. I'll have Ollie bring you some warm oatmeal and a cup of coffee. Does that sound okay?"

"Where's Maddie?" I ask.

"Oh, she slept in Gram's cabin last night. It was kind of a treat for her, and she was exhausted. She doesn't know what happened."

"Maybe she could come by and see me this afternoon," I offer.

"That sounds great. It's going to warm up today, so I'll send over some extra fans, and you can hang out here. Read a book, take your mind off things, okay?"

"Sure," I say. As soon as Winnie leaves the cabin, I crawl back under the covers and breathe slowly through the sheets. I feel shaky and start to cry again. It would be easy to pack up and go home now, and no one would blame me. But I know going home won't really solve anything. I pick up the phone. On the third ring, Keegan picks up.

There's a knock on the door. It's Ollie with a tray of oatmeal, grapefruit, toast, and coffee. It smells good and my stomach growls with acknowledgment.

"Are you okay?" he asks, looking at the pile of tissues on the bed and my blotchy face. I sit up as he places the tray on the bedside table.

"I guess. Just got off the phone with my brother. He was pretty upset."

"I can imagine." Ollie pulls out a small bag of brown sugar from his pocket. "Gram said you like your coffee black, so here's a little sugar for the oatmeal."

"Thanks." I take it from him and scoop a spoonful over the warm mush in the bowl.

"What are you going to do?" he asks.

"Right now?" I ask, and he nods.

"Eat." I try for a bit of a smile. "My brother thinks I should come home, but I'm not sure that's the best thing for me. I don't know what my mom thinks I should do." I pause, considering how much to share. "She's not like Winnie," I explain.

"Not many moms are like Winnie," he offers. I nod in agreement.

I hate how worried Ollie looks. I catch his eyes. "What happened last night, it was awful, but I'm okay," I say softly.

He's silent for a moment. "I'm glad." He concentrates on my face. It looks like he's searching for something.

"What?" I ask.

A faint blush blooms along his freckles. "I'm not sure. I'm surprised, that's all. I didn't think you would want to stay here anymore." He looks like a little kid for a second, and I can picture him at Maddie's age.

"I don't know. I feel like I haven't been following my instincts very well lately. My gut tells me I should stay, so for now, I'm going with that."

"Maddie will be glad."

"Just Maddie?" I prod. I can't help myself.

"No, and mom and Gram. All of us," he says softly. Then silence.

"Thanks for breakfast."

"You're welcome. I'll be back to check on you later this afternoon. Maybe I'll bring Maddie by for a game of Scrabble."

I nod and he gets up from the bed and moves to the door.

"Ring the bell if you need something."

"The bell?" I ask.

"Yeah, on your tray." He points and I see a small silver bell with the letter "W" engraved on it.

"Thanks." I swear the bell appeared out of thin air. How nice, and kind of silly, since there's no way he could actually hear the tiny bell outside my cabin. But when I look up to say something, he isn't there. Oh well. It was nice to talk to him. I wonder if Jonathan will stop in, but I doubt it. He has his stuff to deal with today. Last night he seemed pretty out of control.

I feel empty all of a sudden and dive into breakfast. When I've worked my way through most of it, I pull out my sketchbook. My drawings look stiff and stilted. I flip through them and start over on a fresh page. When I finish, my face stares back at me. In the background, I sketch the cabin, the lake, and a boat. I add a child in the woods.

By midafternoon there's another knock on the door. I startle out of my daze. My hands are covered with charcoal, and my bed is quilted with pictures.

"Just a minute," I call, and give a swift sweep of the pictures, piling them into the drawing pad. I brush my bangs from my eyes and walk to the door.

"Hello," I say, as Maddie bursts into the room and hugs me around the waist.

"You don't look sick," she says, matter-of-fact, and I giggle.

"Well, you don't look tired either, but I bet you are! What time did you get to bed, little Miss Maddie? Two in the morning? Midnight?" I poke her gently in the ribs, and she grabs my hand to stop me. Ollie is right behind her carrying the Scrabble game close to his chest.

"Working with charcoal today?" he asks.

"What?"

He points to my forehead. I look in the mirror on the dresser and see a big black mark on my skin. "Oh! Yeah. Let me go wash my hands. You can set up the game over there," I say, heading towards the bathroom and pointing at the small card table in the corner of the room. I scrub my hands and my face, and when I return, Ollie has organized the game and pulled up a couple of extra chairs.

"Who else is coming?" I ask, anticipating the possible answers.

"Oh, we invited Gram to join us," Ollie says. "Hope you don't mind."

"No, that would be great." On cue, Gram comes through the door wearing a white tennis skirt and a collared short-sleeve top. Her hair tied up in a yellow scarf. She looks like a pro. Her legs are as buff as Ollie's.

"Hi, Gram," I say.

"Leda, let me look at you. Are you feeling better?" she asks.

"Yes, a bit. It's been nice to have a quiet day in the cabin."

"Well, this doesn't seem very quiet, does it?" Gram gives Maddie a warning look. She's bumping her chair up and down.

We play for hours. Everyone takes a turn helping Maddie with her letters. Ollie is quite good at coming up with unusual words, but Gram creams us. She's a master. We play again. Before I know it, the afternoon has drifted by.

21

✦

Jonathan Tanner-Eales
SUPPORT

OM WAITED on my porch for me to surface this morning, but I didn't want to talk. At least not to her. I texted Ricky to tell him I missed him. I wanted to share what happened last night. No response.

I wander around the property and find my way to the kitchen for a late lunch. I'm walking past Leda's cabin on my way back when I hear laughter and giggling coming through the door. Leda's clearly having fun with Ollie, Gram, and Maddie. I expected her to be sadder today.

I pause. "That was a fun game, but I think this little one needs a snack," I hear Gram say, and then there's shuffling and what sounds like pieces of a game being tossed into a box. Gram and Maddie exit the creaky screen door, and Gram smiles at me as they leave. I approach the door but hear Ollie talking to Leda, so I stand quietly on the porch.

"Why don't you chill for a while," he says. "I'll come and get you in time for dinner if you want."

"Do you think Marcia and Jonathan will be there?" she asks.

"I'm not sure. I think Marcia is planning to go back home."

I reach up and knock on the door. "Can I come in?" I ask. Ollie walks over and pushes the door open for me.

"Hey," Leda says. She's sitting on her bed. Fans blow in all directions, making the curtains wave.

"I was just getting ready to go," Ollie says. "Do you want company?" he asks Leda. She shakes her head no and he moves out the door.

"See you soon," he says to me—I guess a hint that I should keep my visit short.

"Sure," I say. I watch him cross the deck and disappear down the stairs. I slide my hands into my pockets and feel for my phone. I wonder if Ricky's responded to my text yet.

"I wanted to thank you—" Leda begins, but I cut her off. She looks nervous. Probably afraid I'm going to lose it again.

"No, you don't have to thank me. I just wanted to see if you're okay."

She's rubbing at black stains on her fingers, making eye contact in little bursts. "Yeah, I'm okay," she says. "Shaken up. It was pretty scary."

"I know," I say.

"Do you want to talk about it?" she asks.

"Not really," I say, but I sit down at the card table anyway. Leda gets off the bed, walks over to the table, and sits across from me. She looks at me oddly and reaches a hand out to the middle of the table. She gestures for me to hold it, and surprisingly, I do. I feel an urge to share with her. "It's hard. Being at the water. I never really stop thinking about it."

Leda squeezes my hand. It's hot in here and I'm sweating. "I'm sorry," she says. She seems calm as the lake.

I shrug. It's not her fault, really.

But she keeps talking steadily. "Jonathan, I didn't know what they were going to do. That night, we were going to swim, but then you were there . . . with Ricky."

I look up at her. "You were there?" I whisper, and she nods. So many feelings soup together in my gut.

"Jonathan," Leda whispers back, "I'm sorry I didn't tell the truth. I was afraid what would happen. I didn't know what they were going to do, and then I was scared of what David would do if I told."

I stare at Leda, confused. She knew that whole time? "What do you mean? You were afraid he'd hurt you?'" I ask.

"My mom . . ." she hesitates, then screws up her face and plunges on, "she sells. Stuff that would get her in trouble. And David knows. I was worried he'd tell the cops if I didn't back him up," Leda says.

She's telling the truth. "Okay," I say, "Wow. Why are you telling me now?" This means nothing unless she's willing to say it in court.

Leda gets up from the chair and walks over to her sketchbook. She pulls out a drawing of a woman with long, gray hair. She has Leda's eyes and is sitting alone on a stool in an empty room. She hands the picture to me. "I talked to my brother this morning. Mom's going to turn herself in. She knows things that will help her get a good deal—she has a connection to a guy, a doctor, they've been trying to charge for a while. She's going to help."

"And your mother? What's going to happen to her?" I ask.

"Keegan said she'll probably be given a reduced sentence, or just probation and community service if she's cooperative." Leda inhales and exhales. She looks unbearably sad. "I didn't know what to do, Jonathan. I was in the truck. I heard you and Ricky screaming, and I got scared and ran."

I stare at the picture of her mother. I'm confused, and relieved, and validated. But this doesn't change anything. "Thanks for telling the truth," I say. "I hope things turn out okay for your mom." Leda takes this in and quietly moves back to her bed. She perches on the edge of the blanket. I want to grab her and make her promise to testify against David. I want her to sign something in writing. I want her to call Ricky, the newspapers, the school. I want to force her to do all those things, right this very moment, but I don't. I imagine this day has been exhausting for her. It can wait. So I stand up instead and carry the picture of her mother to the dresser and tuck it back into the folder. Out of her view.

"Get some rest," I suggest, stepping out of the cabin, closing the door quietly, and move towards the kitchen.

My phone buzzes in my pocket, and I see Alan

Norton's name. I hold up the phone and reroute towards my cabin.

"Hello?" I answer.

"Jonathan," Alan's voice breaks, "I'm afraid I have some bad news."

22

✦

Jonathan Tanner-Eales

FAITH IN TOGETHERNESS

I CLUTCH THE PHONE. This is too much.

"What happened?" My ears are pounding.

"He's okay. Ricky swallowed a lot of pills," his father chokes. "He's alive, but he's back in the hospital."

I sit on the ground, my arms and legs shaking. The smell of the lake, the night air.

I go straight to the hospital. The clouds cast a shadow that blankets my heart. I imagine Ricky hooked up to monitors and tubes, like he was back in May, but when I walk into his room he's standing by the window, looking out at a playground. I stand next to him. There's a father pushing his child on the swings.

"Ricky," I say. He turns to look at me. His eyes are

dull and his hair is greasy. He wears a pair of green hospital pants and a white T-shirt.

"I came as soon as I could." He doesn't respond, just shifts his eyes to the wall behind my head. "You look really good, though," I continue, trying to sound encouraging, but my voice sounds far away. I'm unable to pull my gaze from the scar across his left eyebrow. I feel awkward, like we're on a first date and things aren't going well.

"Thanks, so do you. Looks like you did a lot of swimming at the lake." The words hang in the air. Ricky continues on, "Listen, I don't blame you, okay?"

I don't say anything. He continues. "I know you couldn't have stopped them on your own. I froze up; I shut down. There was nothing you could have done on your own." Ricky is steady. He isn't emotional, just matter-of-fact.

"But I should have tried," I whisper. "I should have gotten out of the water and tried, and instead I just swam away and watched them hurt you." I want to move toward him and hold him, but I'm scared. Instead I sit down on the corner of the empty bed. Ricky stays at the window. He's turns his gaze out to the swing set again.

"And if you had gotten out of the water and tried to help, then what? What do you think they would have done to you? No. Then we'd both have been messed up, and I might have died."

For a long moment, I take in his words, staring at my feet, feeling like I failed again. It's too hard to think about Ricky's death. And here we are, back in the hospital, because he wanted to die.

"Why did you take those pills?" I blurt out, but I sound angry and regret my tone immediately. Ricky turns to face me. He looks almost embarrassed, but then his face softens. I look at the floor, tears welling up, feeling ashamed.

"Every time I looked in the mirror I saw this kid who was weak, who was a victim, who couldn't fight back, and I didn't want to be him anymore. I didn't want to be here." His voice is still steady.

"And now?" I ask, unsure if I'm ready for his answer.

"I regretted it almost as soon as I did it. I realized that I was giving up on myself. It's weird. I was always worried about being gay around my family, and after that night and the media, well, it's just out there. No one can pretend anymore. Like now they're on my side, and they don't seem to mind so much." Ricky hesitates, so I prepare to tell him all the reasons he shouldn't give up on himself. I take a deep breath, but he cuts me off before I can speak. "My family isn't giving up on me. But that's how I saw myself . . . After they pumped my stomach, I talked to the psychiatrist for a long time."

"About that night?"

"About everything: what's happened at school, at the reservoir, and taking the pills. It's helped. A lot."

"I'm glad," I whisper, tears now leaking from my eyes.

"And you know what my dad's been doing?" Ricky asks.

"What?" I have no idea what he's about to say.

"He asked me to make a list of kids I know from school who could have heard David and MJ harass me before, and then he went door-to-door and spoke with their parents and got them to talk with their kids about testifying on our behalf."

"That's great, Ricky," I say. "Who has he talked to?"

"Oh, the usual, kids we've taken classes with. Even Leda's mom."

"Leda?" I'm surprised. "What did her mom say?"

"Well, she was defensive at first. I think she really likes David, though I can't understand why," Ricky smiles. "I like Leda. I tried to call her myself, but I guess she went away for the summer, to some lake to be a nanny or something."

"Yeah, I saw her there . . . I mean, she was at my cousin's camp, working," I reply.

Ricky's eyes open wide. "Really? Did you talk with her?"

I nod my head. "A little," I say, thinking about all that happened in just a few days. "She was there, at the reservoir with David and MJ, but she ran away." I pause, giving Ricky a moment to let this sink in before I continue. "I think she's going to tell the truth," I finish, reaching over to lay a hand on Ricky's arm. He feels solid and warm and alive.

His eyes open wider. "Really? Then we'll have an eyewitness."

"I know. I have an appointment with the attorney tomorrow, to go over everything," I say, stepping closer to Ricky, sitting next to him in a straight-backed chair. "I need to talk to Leda again too."

"Good." He grows quiet. "I'm not going back to Mount Lincoln."

I'm startled. "What do you mean?"

"I don't want to be there anymore, not with all of those kids staring at my scars. I don't want to be the gay kid who got beat up until I graduate," he says.

"But they're testifying for us. You have friends there."

"Not really. And without you there, I just can't."

"But where will you go?"

"I'm going to a private school in Montpelier. My dad works near there, so he can drive me in." He changes gears. "What about you? Are you still going to Emerson?" He sounds hopeful.

"I'm requesting a deferment to start in January, but yeah, I'm still going. I'm moving in with my dad after this is over, until the term begins."

"You're moving back to Boston?" His face drops, and I can tell I've hurt him again.

"Not right away, but hey, you've got a place to stay when you come down to visit schools, right?"

"Right," he says, and we're silent for a long moment. He walks over to the bed and sits on the edge next to me. He flexes his feet and rubs his hands together. "I'm sorry I asked you to go away," Ricky says, and he reaches into a drawer and pulls out a diary. "I've been writing down my memories, about that night and the past year. You're so much a part of my life—" He breaks off and opens the journal to his neat print. "I can't really say everything I want to say. Maybe you can just read this." He offers me the book and I take it, feeling uneasy, but honored.

"I don't know, Ricky, are you sure you want me to read this?" I ask, and he nods, and then lies down, turning his back to me.

23

✦

Leda Keogh

SPLITTING

KEEGAN MEETS ME at the bus stop in Burlington and drives me the hour and a half home. His green eyes scan me from head to toe.

"You look okay," he states, reassuring himself.

"I *am* okay," I affirm as he hugs me. And then he kisses the light bruise that remains on my forehead. Weird but appreciated.

As we go speeding through the winding back roads, past the fields and farms, I begin to feel the familiarity of coming home—even though it's just for the weekend. Keegan's wearing a pressed blue dress shirt and khaki pants, and he seems weirdly upbeat and positive.

"Did you talk to the attorney?" Keegan asks.

"Not yet. Why are you so dressed up?" Does he have a girlfriend? I've never seen him so cleaned up.

"New job," he says, keeping his eyes on the road.

"You do? What kind of a job? How come you didn't tell me?" I ask. Keegan is grinning now, and looks extremely pleased with himself.

"I'm the new manager at the Country Store," he says. I'm stunned, and he looks over, laughing. "We need the money now that Mom's going to be doing community service. I want to keep the house so you can finish school. It pays pretty well, better than minimum wage at least."

"How on earth did you ever get that job?" I ask.

"Thanks," he says, smiling at my teasing. "But seriously, why haven't you talked to the attorney?"

"I just have to talk to David first," I say, inhaling in anticipation of Keegan's reaction. I plunge forward. "I heard from Kira that David and MJ hired an attorney too."

"Why do you need to talk to David?" Keegan asks, casting a concerned glance at me. "Has he tried to get in touch with you?"

"Yeah, he called and texted."

"You don't owe him anything, Leda," Keegan says.

"Look, I just need to see him, that's all. I haven't changed my mind. I just want him to hear it from me first," I say nervously. We speed down the road for a few miles, warm air blowing through the opened windows.

Keegan breaks the moment. "Are you going to see Ricky while you're home?"

I hope so. "Jonathan said Ricky is only allowed a few visitors a day, but I'm definitely going to stop by."

"Yeah, good," Keegan says.

"How's Mom, anyway?" I ask, hoping to change the

subject. I haven't had a real conversation with Mom since she turned herself in.

"She's doing okay." I feel a wave of guilt rise up and flush my neck and cheeks. "She's lucky, really. She only had to spend three days in jail, and then they released her to my custody."

"To yours? That's weird." Keegan left these details out of our last call.

"Well, it was either me or more time in jail. Besides, I'm an upstanding citizen with a respectable job," he grins.

"Must be," I smile back.

Charlie's Pizza Pub is empty for an early Saturday afternoon. Two people are sitting at the bar, and a family with small children is in a booth. I was hoping for more of a crowd. I select a booth next to the door, where I can keep my back to the wall and watch for David's arrival. A perky waitress in jeans and a Charlie's Pizza T-shirt steps forward as soon as I slide onto the red vinyl seat.

"Just one today?" she asks.

"No, two," I say. I hear the bells on the door jingle as it opens. I look past her and see David walking towards us. He stares straight at me and doesn't blink, and for a moment I think I've made a mistake. My brother's warning echoes in my ears. He offered to come with me, but I told him no. The waitress places a second napkin in front of David as he sits.

"What can I get you to drink?" she asks.

"Two Dr. Peppers," David says. It's our usual drink order.

"Actually, I'll have an ice tea. Thanks," I say, and David raises his eyebrows but doesn't say anything.

"Okay, that'll be one Dr. Pepper and an ice tea," she repeats. "I'll give you a few minutes with the menu," and she points to the plastic menu in the wire holder up against the wall. David pulls the menu out. Once the waitress leaves, he pushes the menu away and looks at me. My hands feel a little shaky, so I drop them onto my lap. I don't want him to see that I'm scared. This isn't how I'd imagined it in my head. I was braver.

"So, you asked me to come here. What do you want?" David asks.

"I wanted to see how you are." This is a lie.

"Right. Like you give a shit how I am. You've been gone all summer, and you don't take my calls anymore." His voice is tight and controlled.

"Kira told me that you hired a lawyer."

"Had to, looks like they're going to take it to court." He glances around the room. The waitress returns to the table with our drinks.

"Are you ready to order?" she asks.

"Want anything?" I ask David. "I'll buy," I offer, and he gives me a strange look.

"I'll have a personal pepperoni," he tells the waitress, who then turns to me. I ask for the same. The break in conversation gives me the opportunity to take a few silent deep breaths. *Pull it together, Leda.*

"He'll be contacting you," David says.

"Who?" I ask, and then realize that he means his attorney. "Oh, right." David shakes his head.

"About that," I say, "It's just. . ." I pause, thinking about the right words. What sounded so confident and baddass in my head last night seems lame now.

"Just what, Leda?" he asks. "You can't back out now. We'll subpoena you if we have to."

"No, I'm going to testify, but I've already been asked, by the prosecutor," I spit the words out quickly.

"What? Why? What did you tell them?" His eyes narrow and a deep line forms across his forehead. He's so good-looking, but I feel somehow freed from his pull. I can see him objectively. I look at the faint scar above his lip. I used to think it was hot, but now it just reminds me of the scars he left on Ricky.

"I haven't told them anything." I raise my tea to my lips and take a sip, keeping my eyes on his. Something has shifted. I have the power now.

"You don't have a choice, Leda," he says, and breathes out roughly. "Leda, I know so much about your mom. Don't make me do this." He sits back in the booth. He's trying to look concerned, but it comes out as smug. Our food arrives. The waitress doesn't notice the tension and tells us to enjoy. I take a bite of my pizza and chew slowly. David scarfs down a corner of his pizza with just a few bites.

"I don't know if you've heard yet, but my mother turned herself in," I say, and David pulls the slice of pizza away and looks at me.

"What?" he grunts.

"To the police. She told her boss, and she told the police. She's doing community service now." At least part of this is true.

"No fucking way." he almost laughs at the irony.

"Okay. So that means you think you can walk all over me?" Red blotches creep up his neck, and I know he's angry now.

"Look, David. I just wanted to tell you in person, before court. I thought it was only fair, because of everything we've been through..." My words trail off in a whisper. David picks up the tin pizza plate and slams it against the wall. It bends. There's pizza everywhere. The waitress comes over in a hurry.

"Is something wrong? Was the food okay?" she asks, a worried expression on her face.

"It's fucking great," David says, and he walks out of the restaurant.

24

✦

Jonathan Tanner-Eales
STANDING

T HE FIRST WEEK of August, Ricky is finally released from the hospital. We pull into the parking lot of the general store and see Kira and a few other girls getting out of the car next us. Kira hesitates near her door, like she might want to climb back into her car to wait for us to leave. As we unbuckle our seatbelts, the girls quickly move inside the store.

"Come on," I say, seeing the look on Ricky's face. "Let's just go inside. We can ignore them." I open my door and he follows, pulling his baseball cap down over his face.

The shelves of the store are tall and the aisles are narrow to accommodate the endless variety of stuff for sale. The General Store has everything from groceries to soft serve to hardware supplies. The nearest grocery store is almost an hour away, so everyone comes here. Kira and her friends are in the snack aisle, and one of them wanders out when the bell on the door announces our entrance. We head over to the drink aisle first, then we'll grab the milk and eggs Mrs. Norton asked us to pick up. I think she was just trying to get us out of the house, where we spend a lot of time watching videos, kicking a soccer ball around, and eating.

"Don't," I hear one of them plead. They clearly have some issue with us, but I don't care. This is a free country. I grab our items, plus Reese's Cups for the ride home, and head towards check out, Ricky close on my heels.

David Slayton steps out from the aisle. The girls are close behind him. My whole body turns cold, and I can hear my heart pounding in my ears. I stop in my tracks and look him in the eyes. I hear a funny noise escape from Ricky behind me, and I see David try to catch a glimpse of him. The hair on my arms is standing up, but I steady myself and square my shoulders.

"Is there a problem here, boys?" Keegan Keogh moves from behind the counter and steps towards us, locking eyes with David. He places himself near my left shoulder, towering above us all.

David considers his options. Then he shifts his body and takes a step back. "No," he replies.

"Good," Keegan says. He turns to me, "Are you ready to check out?"

"Yeah." I grab Ricky by the elbow and move him in front of me towards the counter. Keegan begins to scan and bags up our items.

"It's good to see you," he says, looking directly at Ricky.

"Thanks," Ricky says.

"You're Leda's brother, right?" I ask.

"Yup," he says.

"Tell her we say hello, will you?" I say, and Keegan nods and smiles.

"Sure."

25

✦

Leda Keogh

FAMILY

EVER SINCE returning to camp, I have been a jumble of feelings. Knowing that I'll have to confront David's anger again at court makes my stomach clench with fear. Plus, MJ and other kids from school will be there, and I'll have to face them once and for all. It feels so huge, but I try to push it aside and concentrate on being at the lake. I want to enjoy what little time is left. I feel sad that I will be leaving soon. I love this family like my own. Maddie has a friend visiting from town and is busy playing with her dolls, so Ollie and I go down to the boathouse.

"Where do you want to go? We can take the sailboat out," he offers.

"How about kayaking to the island again," I suggest, and Ollie agrees.

My arms have gotten pretty strong over the summer and I'm able to keep pace, finally. When we arrive, Ollie pulls the kayaks up onto the island and then drags me by the hand into the lake. I laugh and splash at him. He splashes back and I escape to the deeper water. It's up to my waist now, and the cold seeps into my hips.

Ollie stops splashing and looks at me. It's a strange sort of silence, so I sink down into the water and make a question mark with my eyes. *What?*

He doesn't respond, so I take advantage of the moment and splash him. The spell is broken. He yelps hoarsely and then sputters and wipes his hair back from his eyes. It's dripping over him like a glazed cake. His mouth twitches into a sideways smile.

"Can I kiss you?" he says.

The universe stops.

Ollie wants to kiss me?

Ollie wants to kiss me.

The universe starts up again.

I'm probably blushing furiously and can't seem to speak, so I do the only thing I'm physically able to: I nod.

Ollie face breaks apart. He grins toothily. "Okay, good." He looks ebullient. And relieved. He moves towards me, reaching ahead and pulling back through the water. He's in front of me now. Honestly, his eyes look like magic. And then he leans in and touches his lips to mine, and I swear, his mouth is the warmth of the sun. And then he presses deeper into me, and it feels like a dark summer storm, and then, oh god, his hand is against the back of my head and I can feel the pressure of his thumb and it feels like everything good in the world.

Wait, what are we doing? I pull back. "What are we doing?" I mean it to sound critical, but it comes out philosophical.

He pulls back too. He looks magnificent. "I've been wanting to do that for a month."

I laugh and lean in to kiss him again—I can't help it. This time it's slow and steady, deliberate even. When I pull back he holds me softly against him, and I can feel the warmth blooming from his neck. I breath in. He smells like lake water and suntan lotion. I reach my hand into the water and splash his back. He yelps and collapses, pulling me into the water with him.

Ollie springs up spitting and laughing. I take off swimming. I can feel him brush against me as I turn in the water to swim back to shore. He follows. When I reach the huge boulders that hug the shoreline, I climb up into the warm sun and stretch out on my back. He does the same.

"When do you go back to school?" I blurt. *Shut up, Leda.* But I'm trying to keep my mind grounded on the reality that this will not be a relationship. I'm about to leave to go back to my regular life.

"I leave in two weeks. We'll pack up the camp this weekend, and then I'll be at home."

"Might you be . . . anywhere near Mount Lincoln during those two weeks?" I ask, and look up at him. I feel a little desperate. I don't want him to slip away, but I know he's under no obligation to see me again. It was just a kiss.

"Why? Is there someone special in Mount Lincoln?"

"Thanks a lot," I say, and elbow him in the ribs. He turns onto his side. With his index finger, he traces the line of my chin. He stops on my bottom lip. His dark eyes are like the evening.

"Leda . . ." he says.

I look away, blushing, and ready for his kind excuse. The limbs of the trees are swaying in the wind as if they are rooting us.

"What are you thinking?" he asks.

Please don't crush my heart, Ollie. "I don't know," I hesitate. "You going back to college."

"So you can forget about me?"

"What?" I ask.

"I'll just be some boring lawyer, getting rich off other people's miserable lives," he says. I smile at this, but don't take my eyes off him.

"What do you want from me, Ollie?" I ask.

"Leda," he says again, "I just want to see you more. Of course I want to come to Mount Lincoln."

"Really?" A smile is forming I can't contain.

"Really," he says. Then he is kissing me again, on my lips and my neck, and when he stops, I can't breathe.

When we return from the island, Ollie's father is actually sitting on my porch. He is Ollie with salt and pepper hair and wrinkled eyes. His pale skin betrays how little he's seen the sun this summer. Ollie looks pleased to see his father out in the sunlight. I expect him to release my hand as we approach, but instead he just squeezes it tighter, making my heart skip. Mr. Woodruff stands, holding an envelope, a serious expression on his face. Am I in trouble again?

"This came for you, Leda." He holds the envelope out, so I reach to receive it, my hand shaking slightly. I pull out a subpoena to testify for the prosecution, and my stomach lurches. The bliss that I felt earlier seems like a distant memory. David's anger looms large in my memory, and I can barely hold the envelope.

"This is it," I whisper. "There's no turning back."

26

✦

Jonathan Tanner-Eales

TIES THAT BIND

WHEN MOM AND I collect our items from the other side of the detectors, we see Ricky's mom and dad at the information desk. Ricky is with them. He looks pale and ghostly, but with a fresh haircut, and shave. He's wearing a clean pair of khakis and a collared shirt. I'm dressed the same, a request by Mr. Burrows. "Dressing respectfully helps," he said, "to win over the hearts of the jury."

The courtroom is flooded with people; every seat is taken. Family, students and teachers from school, and others who, I suppose, are just here for curiosity. The journalists are sitting in the back.

My palms begin to sweat. I search the room and find them: David and MJ, dressed in suits. They're leaning towards each other casually and whispering. They look confident, as if this is an inconvenience and soon they'll be back to their lives. Mr. Burrows is to their right. He steps away from the table to greet us.

"Hi, boys. Now, as we discussed, I'd like the two of you to sit up here at the table with me. That will give the jury the best view of you." He nods toward the group of twelve people who silently sit in a boxed area with neutral expressions. I don't recognize any of them, but I guess that's how it's supposed to be.

I look to Ricky, and we both nod and follow Mr. Burrows down the aisle to the front. I try not to notice David and MJ watching us. I long to hold Ricky's hand. That's what I would do if we were alone; that's what other people would do if they were in this situation.

The judge enters the room and everyone rises. She looks ancient. Every inch of her is wrinkled and she has thick glasses. Her black robe curtains around her legs as she steps up to her post and settles in her seat, glasses sliding down to the end of her long, thin nose. There's a murmur in the audience, and then she strikes her gavel. Everyone shuts up at once and is seated.

Mr. Burrows begins his opening remarks. He is eloquent and speaks passionately about the community holding people responsible for hate crimes. He says that hate crimes hurt the heart of our society. He talks about the importance of morality in our young people, and the need for fairness. He likens Ricky's and my position to that of any other minority in this country.

When he finishes, it is silent. There's hardly the noise of shifting bodies or the mutter of a cough. Now David and MJ's attorney speaks. He pushes the jury to look closely at the young men before them. He reminds them of their own youths, when they had so much to look forward to in life. He says that people make stupid mistakes and end up at the wrong places at the wrong time.

Then Ricky is on the stand. He swears to tell the truth. He's shaking—not just his voice, but his hands. My jaw is clenched and I stare at his face, willing him to look at just me, no one else. We talked about this before the trial. "Don't look at them. Look at me. I'll help you focus," I promised. Ricky can get through this. His eyes find mine and I nod encouragingly.

"I heard a gunshot, and I remember thinking we were both going to die, and then Jonathan grabbed me and pulled me toward the water," he says.

"And then what happened?" Mr. Burrows asks.

"And then everything went black."

"Were you struck in the head?"

"I don't know. I do have a scar on my head, but at that point I have no memory. I woke up in the hospital."

"How many days later?" Mr. Burrows asks.

"Seven."

"You were unconscious for seven days?"

"Well, the doctors said my brain was functioning, but psychologically I was not feeling safe, so I stayed unconscious longer as a way of protecting myself." There are murmurs in the audience, but Ricky keeps his gaze on me.

"You were recently readmitted to the hospital. Can you tell us why?"

Ricky shifts in his seat, looking uncomfortable. "I took some pills, because I didn't want to live anymore." He pauses and takes a deep breath. Someone murmurs from the back of the courtroom and the judge taps her gavel.

"Quiet, please," she demands. She turns to Ricky. "Continue."

"I've struggled with depression since I was little, because I felt different than everyone else. Other kids called me names."

"What names?" Mr. Burrows asks.

"Queer, fag, fairy," Ricky responds. "I try to ignore them. Someone drew pictures of, um, penises, on my notebook covers and I spent hours one day afraid to leave the bathroom stall because someone kept hitting the door to the stall and shouting I was a pussy. I was already scared most of the time of getting hurt, but after that night at the reservoir, it felt like too much. Like there was no way for me to live a normal life." He's quiet for a long moment.

Mr. Burrows' voice is gentle as he encourages Ricky to continue.

"I can't go back to that school," Ricky says.

"Why?" The attorney asks. Ricky shifts his eyes to David and MJ.

"I don't want to be around people like that."

Then a doctor is put on the stand and he describes Ricky's injuries and his recovery process. Lots of questions about his diagnosis of PTSD are asked and the doctor responds in detail. Next Mr. Burrows calls for Officer Templeton to enter the courtroom and take the stand. She's dressed in full uniform, her hair braided tightly, and a ring around her forehead shows where her cap would be. She smiles at me and Ricky and then turns her attention to being sworn in. Her testimony lays out the evidence in a thoughtful way, and it leaves me feeling hopeful. Then David's attorney begins his cross-examination. It feels like he's poked holes in all of the circumstantial evidence and the case is deflating.

Then it's my turn. It's nearly lunchtime. Everyone seems restless, but when I reach the stand I see people sitting up a little straighter, or leaning to the left or right to get a better look. From this vantage point I can see some of my classmates in the audience. Most of them are friends, but not all. Ricky's father has one arm wrapped around himself, and the other is gripping the bench. He's looking at the floor. Is he mortified that Ricky's life is on display? This is so public.

In the back of the courtroom is my mother. She's wearing a pair of jeans and a white shirt, her hair pulled back. She looks tired. Dark circles deepen under her eyes, and her skin is pale. I feel as if I'm looking at her for the first time since that night. Our eyes meet, and she nods and gives me a smile of encouragement.

"Can you describe the night of May eighteenth of this year?" Mr. Burrows asks. The silence of the courtroom swallows my bravery like a fish. I try to begin but my voice falters. I force myself to keep going. *I can do this.* It's like being on stage. I recount what happened. I describe hearing the gunfire and feeling Ricky freeze up. I describe not being able to get him to move or swim away. I describe the feeling of Ricky being torn from my hands.

Mr. Burrows waits until I'm done. "Are the people who attacked you in this courtroom?"

"Yes," I answer. "It was David Slayton and Michael James Farrar." I look directly at David, who's lip curls upward into a sneer. Whispers erupt in the room.

"Were you able to see them?" Mr. Burrows asks.

"No." I answer.

"How do you know it was David and Michael that attacked Ricky?"

I look at my hands and then up at the jury. "I know David's voice from the hundreds of times he's called me names at school. I know Michael's voice from when he screams 'pussy' at me in the school bathrooms."

"I see," says Mr. Burrows. "And why didn't you try to make them stop?" I swallow. The room is somber again. We practiced this question.

"I didn't think I could take them both," I say. "I was afraid . . . I was afraid that if I went to shore to try to help, I would only make things worse."

"Meaning?" Mr. Burrows pushes.

"Meaning I'm not a good fighter. I'm not as strong as David or MJ. I do musicals and sing in choir." Someone giggles and the judge smashes her gavel down and insists on order.

The questions continue and I describe everything I remember. When I look for my mom again, I see her wiping her face.

Lunch recess is called and I turn to see Mom moving down the side of the courtroom towards me. She reaches for me and then her arms are wrapped around me and we hug for a long time. I inhale her lily-scented lotion and feel my shoulders relax.

She pulls away, examining my face with concern.

"It's okay, Mom. Don't worry." I force a smile and squeeze her hands.

27

✦

Leda Keogh

BUNDLED

DAVID'S MOTHER tried to reach me by phone. The Slaytons are nothing if not loyal to each other. "He's a good person, Leda. He just gets a little rambunctious, but he didn't mean any harm. Please call me back, so I know you got my message." Instead, I logged on to Verizon to change my number.

I expected the courtroom to be dark and scary, like on television, but this room is brightly lit. The sun makes the maple desktops glow. I hear Mr. Burrows call me to take the stand. I walk slowly across the carpet, my heart beating in my ears. Despite the urge to run the other way, somehow I find myself in the chair to the judge's left, and I look into David's face for first time since our lunch. He looks miserable and pathetic. His eyes are pleading with me, and I flush red with guilt and anger. When I look beyond Mr. Burrows, I see Jonathan. His face is hopeful.

"Can you state your full name for the record?" Mr. Burrows asks.

"Leda Marie Keogh," I say. The acoustics pick up every decibel.

"How do you know David Slayton and Michael James Farrar?"

"David and I dated for almost a year, and Michael is David's best friend, so I saw them both almost every day during the school year," I say.

"Please tell the court what you were doing on the night of May eighteenth."

I steady my breath and plunge forward. "David picked me up after he got out of work, around seven at night. We went to Charlie's to eat, and then we drove around for a little while."

"Did you drive anywhere specific?" Mr. Burrows asks.

"Yes, we went to the reservoir, to go swimming," I say.

"Swimming in May?" Mr. Burrows asks.

I take a deep breath and look out at the audience. Keegan is there, and next to him is Ollie. I almost look away and then realize that on the other side of Keegan is my mom. She's nodding her head encouragingly.

"We went there because it was a hot night and we wanted to skinny dip," I say as matter-of-fact as I can, not looking at David or Ollie, but directly at Mr. Burrows.

"And is that what you did at the reservoir?"

"No," I reply. "When we got there, there was another car parked in the lot. I was pretty sure I knew who it was, so I suggested we leave. But David wanted to see what was going on."

"Who owned the car?"

"I wasn't completely sure, but I thought it was Jonathan's car. Then we saw Jonathan and his boyfriend, Ricky. And David got really angry."

"Why was David angry?"

"Because he doesn't like Jonathan."

"Why?" Mr. Burrows asks.

"Jonathan is gay, and David hates people who are gay."

"How do you know he hates people who are gay?"

"He's told me, and I've seen him pick on Jonathan and Ricky at school."

"Objection, Your Honor, there are no charges of harassment," David's attorney interjects. A murmur springs from the courtroom. The judge crashes her gavel down.

"Keep it moving, Burrows," the judge says.

"Leda, what happened after David got angry?"

"I told David we should just leave, go find someplace else. Jonathan and Ricky were kissing each other."

"How do you know Jonathan Tanner-Eales and Ricky Norton?"

"I took a science class with Ricky; he was my lab partner."

"Had you ever talked to Ricky about his relationship with Jonathan?"

"No, but everyone knows they're dating. They hold hands sometimes, and they walk each other to class."

"What happened then at the reservoir?" Mr. Burrows asks.

"I was holding David's hand, and I felt his whole body tense up when he saw Jonathan and Ricky. He said that he wasn't going to let it happen in his town."

"He called it his town?"

"Yes. He was really upset and started swearing and stormed back to the truck."

"Did the boys in the reservoir hear you?"

"No, I don't think so." I look over at Mr. Norton, who sits upright, staring into the back of David's head.

"And then what happened?"

"David called MJ. Told him what was happening and that he wanted to kick their asses. I tried to stop him, but he just laughed and then he told me if I couldn't play along I should stay in the truck. He was really mad and I was afraid. Then MJ arrived with a shotgun. I told them to just leave the boys alone, and that they weren't hurting anyone. But then David told me they weren't going to really hurt them, just scare them a little, make them jump. It was all in good fun, and they would be right back. He told me to wait in the truck." I swallow, feeling the intensity of the people in the room.

"And did you wait in the truck?" Mr. Burrows asks.

"Yes, at first I did." My eyes are watering. "But it didn't sound like they were just playing a joke. I heard screaming and the gun going off and water splashing and yelling. I was really scared for Ricky and Jonathan, and for myself, so I got out of the truck and ran as far as I could down the road. I got to the Henderson's house and I called my brother, Keegan, and waited for him to come and pick me up."

I look at Jonathan and Ricky. "I'm so sorry," I whisper. "I should have called the police right away. I'm so sorry." There are lots of murmurs in the courtroom, and the judge smashes her gavel again and orders silence.

Ricky and Jonathan are both crying, and Jonathan is rubbing Ricky's back. I feel the heat of David's glare. I don't dare look his way. Instead, I look down to my folded hands on my lap. They're still shaking. There's no turning back. *You did the right thing, it's okay, you did the right thing,* I think over and over, and soon something like relief loosens in my chest.

And then Mr. Burrows is done. The judge orders a ten-minute break and I step into the hallway to get a drink of water. Ollie joins me at the fountain. He circles his arm around me and squeezes.

"You're brave," he says, smiling. "I'm proud of you."

"Thank you," I smile back. People are pouring out of the courtroom to use the restrooms and step outside into the sun. Officer Templeton exits and looks my way. She winks before turning towards the front door for some air. Others smile encouragingly, except for David's mother, who begins to walk towards me. Mr. Slayton redirects her.

Jonathan and Ricky approach. I search their faces for reactions to my testimony. Jonathan immediately wraps his arms around me and gives me a huge hug.

"Thank you," he says. I pull back to look at his face. "I'm sorry I didn't help you sooner."

"I know," he says, smiling. "It's okay."

I turn to look at Ricky. He's thin and his cheeks are still gaunt, but his eyes are brighter than they were in the hospital. He looks almost like the school picture that was in the news, but the scar above his right eye is still red and stands out under his long, blond bangs.

"How are you?" I ask.

"Better," he says. "It's just going to take me a while."

We're called back into court, and David and MJ's attorney is talking quietly with Mr. Burrows and the judge. I'm not sure if I should return to the stand, so I wait in the back of the room. Ollie stops with me and grabs my hand.

The attorneys step back from the bench and the judge pounds her gavel.

"The defense would like to discuss a change in plea in the judge's chambers. Court will adjourn until tomorrow morning at eight," she announces. I turn to Ollie and he hugs me again.

"Maybe it's almost over," he says.

"I hope," I reply. "Come get coffee with me? I have an idea."

28

✦

Leda Keogh

UNBROKEN

MY SENIOR YEAR at Mount Lincoln started the Wednesday before Labor Day and five days after David and MJ pled guilty to harassment and aggravated assault with a deadly weapon. They were sentenced to five years in prison, with three years suspended if they can show good behavior. David, of course, lost his scholarship. I'll have finished with college when they're both be free. Mr. Burrows told Jonathan and Ricky he was surprised a judge gave such a harsh sentence, because in some places in this country, he said, the boys would have only been given community service. I can imagine my mother serving her community service with David and MJ.

The local paper printed every detail they could find on the story, and it was the focus of every conversation at the Country Store, according to Keegan. People couldn't get enough. They couldn't believe a baseball star like David Slayton, headed to play for UCLA, had been caught beating up on some gay kids. Some were appalled with David and MJ's actions, while others seemed more obsessed with the idea that two boys would go to a public place and skinny dip. Keegan said he overheard a woman talk about the influence of having so many gays around on children in the community, and that it wasn't decent. He made several suggestions to her about what should be considered decency. After stories like that, I was dreading going back to school. So, I called Marcia.

"I know Jonathan is getting ready to move, but I wondered if you could help me with something on the first day of school," I say. There's silence at first, but I'm confident she'll be interested. Ever since my testimony, Marcia has been very generous to me, inviting me for dinner and teaching me how to cook. She offered to put me in touch with a few illustrators she knows at various magazines, and I'm working on getting an internship set up for next summer.

"What are you hoping to do?" she asks.

"I want to make the school a more welcoming place the first few days, but I think I need some parental help. And you have some names from when you helped Mr. Norton find witnesses, right?"

Marcia is enthusiastic. I've already spoken to Principal Rafferty, who was more than open to the plan since the high school is under a lot of scrutiny right now. The allegations that students were being regularly harassed and bullied in Mount Lincoln created major migraines for the principal and the staff. And the ACLU of Vermont had some pretty harsh things to say, according to Marcia.

"Let me text you the names, Leda. You should stop by before the weekend is over to say goodbye to Jonathan, I know he'll want to see you. He leaves on Monday."

"Wow, that's so soon! I can't believe he's really going off to college," I say.

"I know, but you'll be down in October to check out schools, right? Ollie said you're planning a visit." Marcia chats a while longer and offers a few suggestions for the tables, and then I set to work.

So here I am, the first day of senior year, a perfect crisp fall day, and I've got two long tables set up in the courtyard of the school. Each is packed with information about every club in school. All of them. I helped make flags for each club and organization, and I color coded them with the days of the week and season they're offered. Every club has at least one member standing by ready to welcome new students, even cheerleading Abbey stepped up to represent the cheer squad.

One whole table is dedicated to the Pride Club. Anita, dressed in jeans and a PFLAG T-shirt, is handing out informational materials and rainbow buttons. She's collecting names of students who are willing to be friendly allies to any person who wants an escort to or from class. She's also starting a "new friend table" at lunch for people who want to talk, or reach out beyond their own friend group.

The first bus arrives and students clamber off, curious but also hesitant to take a look. Thankfully, Kira wastes no time running over to us in an enthusiastic way.

"Look at all of this!" she exclaims. "This is so awesome." And she starts taking pictures and posting them. So by the time the second bus arrives, students already know what to expect. They weave around the tables, grabbing free pins and flags. I even see a guy on the baseball team slip an info sheet into his pocket, and I smile, thinking I should say hey. Maybe he needs an ally.

By the fifth bus we're running low on supplies, and the bell is close to ringing for the start of classes. I'm packing up the materials when I see a new kid, clearly a freshman, reach for the same stack of flyers I'm about to grab.

"Sorry! Here you go," I say, taking a pamphlet out of the stack and placing it in his hand. He has bleach blond hair, chocolate eyes, and a dimple in both cheeks. He's adorable.

"Welcome to Mount Lincoln!" I say, and I offer him my hand to shake. He grins and awkwardly takes my hand.

"Thanks," he says. "I didn't expect to see all this on the first day of school. Especially the Pride table."

"We want you to be comfortable here," I smile happily. "I'm Leda. What's your name?"

"Philip! Can I help you carry any of this into the building?" he offers.

"That would be great!" I say, and the two of us pick up the boxes and walk inside our school.

DISCUSSION GUIDE

✦

Start a conversation about how to be an ally

- Discuss the title of the novel and its significance. Who remembers Aesop Fables from when you were younger?

- Stories have been used for centuries to teach people about morality. What parallels did you see in the fables and Leda and Jonathan's stories?

- What is friendship? Describe the important elements of Leda's relationships with Jonathan, Kira, Ricky, and Ollie. Is she ever really friends with any of them? Can friendship mean something different to different people? Cite different passages in the novel as evidence of your opinion.

- Leda feels caught between speaking up for her friend and turning her boyfriend in to the police. Are her concerns legitimate?

- What keeps Leda in her relationship with David? How do you know when a relationship is healthy?

- What does Jonathan struggle with after the night at the reservoir? How does Ricky help him to manage his guilt?

- The second fable is about persuasion. When can you use the power of persuasion to change someone's mind? How do you know if they will take action just because they change their mind?

- The third fable is about unity. People often feel the need to band together to make their voice heard. How does Leda find her voice? What issues do you feel your community needs to band together to address?

- How do you find the confidence to stand up for what you believe in? What do you need from your peers and your community to feel heard?

- What does it mean to be an ally? What does it mean to have an ally?

RESOURCES

✦

AUTHOR'S WEBSITE: www.sarahwardvt.com

HER "HOW TO BE AN ALLY" WEBSITE:
https://sarahwardvt.com/2017/10/12/
how-to-be-an-ally-join-the-conversation/

www.Itgetsbetter.org

The **It Gets Better Project** inspires people across the globe to share their stories and remind the next generation of LGBTQ+ youth that hope is out there, and it will get better.

www.thetrevorproject.org

Founded in 1998 by the creators of the Academy-Award winning short film *Trevor*, The Trevor Project is the leading national organization that provids crisis intervention and suicide prevention services to lesbian, gay, bisexual, transgender, and questioning (LGBTQ) young people ages 13-24.

www.gladd.org

GLAAD rewrites the script for LGBTQ acceptance. As a dynamic media force, GLAAD tackles tough issues to shape the narrative and provoke dialogue that leads to cultural change. GLAAD protects all that has been accomplished and creates a world where everyone can live the life they love.

ABOUT THE AUTHOR

SARAH WARD writes young adult fiction, poetry and journal articles in the field of child welfare. Over a twenty-five-year career as a social worker, Sarah has worked with young adults and families with harrowing backgrounds. She won the 2007 Editor's Choice Award for the *New England Anthology of Poetry* for her poem "Warmer Waters," and she has been a member of the League of Vermont Writers since 2008. In her limited spare time, Sarah enjoys a good book, a little yoga, and a cup of tea at her home in Williston, Vermont.

ABOUT THE ILLUSTRATOR

LINDSAY L. WARD lives in Williston, Vermon,t with her family. She loves to paint, learn, and stay active in her community. She will be studying illustration for children's books and Spanish at college in Fall, 2018.